"You're going to use the discovery of the bones to launch an investigation into that construction area as a possible burial site for those missing people."

"Exactly." He shook out his uniform shirt and hung it on the back of a kitchen chair. "It won't carry the same weight as a sacred site, but it will definitely cause delays in the construction."

"Does that mean you're not going to tell anyone that I dropped those bones there?"

"Why should I? The interruption you caused will give me some time to poke around that land. Then when forensics discovers the bones are...whatever they are, I'll have another reason to halt the project. Maybe I'll make a similar discovery in Paradiso as we did south of San Diego." He put his finger to his lips. "And you won't tell anyone about my plans, either, right?"

"My lips are sealed."

He stuck out his hand. "Then we have a deal."

"Deal." She curled her hand around his, her smooth flesh sending tingles up his arm.

BURIED
SECRETS

—

CAROL ERICSON

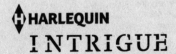

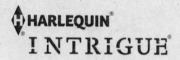

Recycling programs
for this product may
not exist in your area.

ISBN-13: 978-1-335-13600-8

Buried Secrets

Copyright © 2020 by Carol Ericson

All rights reserved. No part of this book may be used or reproduced in
any manner whatsoever without written permission except in the case of
brief quotations embodied in critical articles and reviews.

This is a work of fiction. Names, characters, places and incidents
are either the product of the author's imagination or are used fictitiously.
Any resemblance to actual persons, living or dead, businesses,
companies, events or locales is entirely coincidental.

This edition published by arrangement with Harlequin Books S.A.

For questions and comments about the quality of this book,
please contact us at CustomerService@Harlequin.com.

Harlequin Enterprises ULC
22 Adelaide St. West, 40th Floor
Toronto, Ontario M5H 4E3, Canada
www.Harlequin.com

Printed in U.S.A.

Carol Ericson is a bestselling, award-winning author of more than forty books. She has an eerie fascination for true-crime stories, a love of film noir and a weakness for reality TV, all of which fuel her imagination to create her own tales of murder, mayhem and mystery. To find out more about Carol and her current projects, please visit her website at www.carolericson.com, "where romance flirts with danger."

Books by Carol Ericson

Harlequin Intrigue

Holding the Line

Evasive Action
Chain of Custody
Unraveling Jane Doe
Buried Secrets

Red, White and Built: Delta Force Deliverance

Enemy Infiltration
Undercover Accomplice
Code Conspiracy

Red, White and Built: Pumped Up

Delta Force Defender
Delta Force Daddy
Delta Force Die Hard

Red, White and Built

Locked, Loaded and SEALed
Alpha Bravo SEAL
Bullseye: SEAL
Point Blank SEAL
Secured by the SEAL
Bulletproof SEAL

Her Alibi

Harlequin Intrigue Noir

Toxic

Visit the Author Profile page at Harlequin.com.

CAST OF CHARACTERS

Jolene Nighthawk—A member of the Yaqui tribe, Jolene wants to halt construction of a casino on Yaqui land in the desert. Her father was murdered on that land and she wants answers. But when her former lover shows up looking for answers of his own, he throws her plans and her heart into turmoil.

Sam Cross—He's a Border Patrol agent on a mission to discover the burial ground of some missing people—and to win back the love of his life, Jolene Nighthawk, but he soon discovers that his two goals are intertwined and accomplishing one might lose him the other.

Wade Nighthawk—Jolene's cousin is a mover and shaker within the Yaqui tribe, but when his self-interests trump the interests of the tribe, it results in murder.

Melody Nighthawk—Wade's sister may have some personal challenges, but that doesn't stop her from discovering secrets about the casino's construction...secrets that put her life in danger.

Tucker Bishop—He winds up in the wrong place at the wrong time and pays with his life.

El Gringo Viejo—This notorious drug supplier has been identified and is on the run...or is he?

Chapter One

The dark clouds barreled over the Catalina Mountains, and the skies opened. The rain pelted the highway, steam rising from the scorched asphalt. The first monsoon of the season had hit the Sonoran Desert with a vengeance, gleefully dousing the hot, thirsty landscape.

Jolene slammed on the brakes of her truck, her back wheels fishtailing for a few seconds. She pounded one hand on the steering wheel and shouted. "Learn to drive!"

She couldn't risk getting into an accident right now, not with her cargo. Her cell phone rang from the console, and she glanced down at the display showing her cousin's name before answering and switching to speaker.

"Hey, Wade. What's up?"

"It's Gran."

"Gran, if you're just going to keep borrowing Wade's phone, why not let me get you one of your own?"

"I don't know why I just can't get my old phone back." Gran clicked her tongue. "This is not progress."

Jolene twisted her lips. "Landline phones were discontinued on the reservation, Gran. They figured everyone had a cell phone."

"They figured wrong." She coughed.

"Are you still congested?"

"It's nothing. I called to find out when you were coming over. Wade told me you left town for a few days."

Her pulse picked up speed. "What's wrong?"

"Nothing's wrong. Does something always have to be wrong? I just wanted to visit with one of my favorite granddaughters. Where did you go?"

Jolene took a sip of water from the bottle in her cup holder. "I was in… Phoenix, visiting friends."

"Rain's rolling in." Gran sighed. "I felt it in my bones two days ago."

"It's already hit up here, confounding all the drivers from out of state. I'm just south of Tucson, so it's following me down to Paradiso." She cranked on her defroster. "It's going to be a good soaking."

"Well, you keep track of those weather patterns more than I do." Gran sniffed and said something to someone in the background—probably Jolene's cousin Wade. "There have been a few changes in town since you left."

Jolene rolled her eyes. Gran loved to gossip. "In two days? I doubt that, Gran."

"You know that young Border Patrol agent, Rob Valdez?"

"Pretty face, pumped-up arms? Yeah, I know Rob."

"He's off the market."

"What market would that be, Gran?" Jolene clamped her mouth closed against the laugh bubbling against her lips. She knew exactly which market Gran meant.

Gran huffed out a breath. "The marriage market, Jolene. He and some young woman left on an extended vacation together."

"A vacation? You're kidding. That seals his fate right there. He might as well attach a ball and chain to his ankle."

"Oh, you can laugh, but he was an eligible bachelor, one of the few left in town."

"Nice guy, but not my type. Too young for one thing."

"I know your type, Jolene, and the loss of Rob isn't so bad given the other news I picked up while you were gone."

Jolene's jaw tightened for a second. "Don't keep me in suspense, Gran. What is this other blessed event that occurred to counteract Rob Valdez's vacation with a woman?"

Gran paused for maximum dramatic effect. "Sam Cross is back in town."

Jolene's hands jerked on the steering wheel, and a wall of water from the puddle she'd veered into washed over the side of her truck. She swallowed. "Sam's back?"

"I know Sam *is* your type."

Jolene gripped the steering wheel. "Sam is married. That is most certainly *not* my type."

"He's divorced." Gran moved the phone from her mouth and yelled, "Just a few more minutes, Wade."

Jolene snorted. "He's been back for two days, and you already know his marital status? I doubt it, Gran. He would never leave his daughter."

"He had lunch at Rosita's yesterday, and Rosie told me he wasn't wearing a wedding band and when she asked to see pictures of his daughter, he showed her pictures on his phone of the girl but none of his wife."

Tears stung Jolene's eyes, and she blinked them away. "That's it, then. No wedding ring and no pics of the wife. You and Rosie are quite the spies."

Gran lowered her voice. "You don't have to pretend with me, Jolene."

"Sounds like Wade wants his phone back."

Jolene cleared her throat of the lump lodged there and said, "I'll drop by the rez tomorrow. I have something to do tonight when I get home."

"Drive carefully and come over any time tomorrow." Gran must've handed the phone back to Wade without hanging up, as voices floated over the line before Wade cut off the call.

Jolene blew out a long breath. What was Sam doing in town? It must have to do with work. He wouldn't be in Paradiso long, and she could probably avoid seeing him. She hoped she could avoid seeing him.

She drove the rest of the way to Paradiso hunched over the steering wheel, the rain not putting her on edge as much as the task before her. She could do it. She *had* to do it. As her father had taught her, sometimes the ends did justify the means.

Twenty minutes later, as she rolled into Paradiso, the rain came in with her, lashing through the town, flooding the streets. By the time she pulled into her driveway, the storm had spent itself with the dark clouds rushing across the desert and breaking apart at the border, as if an invisible wall existed there.

She pressed her thumb against the remote-control button in her truck that rolled back the garage door. She slid from the vehicle and took a quick glance around her neighborhood before opening the back door of the cab. She pulled out her overnight suitcase and set it on the ground, and then she grabbed the duffel bag on the back seat with both hands and hauled it from the truck.

She hitched the strap of the bag over her shoulder and lugged it into her garage, wheeling the suitcase behind her. She stashed the duffel under a counter next to her ski boots and bindings, nudging it into place with the toe of her wet sneaker.

She locked her truck and closed the garage door, standing still in the middle of her garage for several seconds until the automatic lights went out. Her eyes picked out the duffel bag in the dim confines of the garage, and then she spun around and charged through the door connecting her garage to her kitchen.

There was no turning back now.

She unpacked her suitcase. She hadn't lied to Gran about spending a few nights away, but she'd been in Tucson, not Phoenix. Nobody needed to know where she'd been.

After she unpacked, she searched through her kitchen for suitable dinner fare and ended up grazing on hummus, crackers, a stale flour tortilla and a handful of trail mix.

She watched the time on her cell phone and the rain outside the window. When the digital numbers ticked over to ten o'clock and the remainder of the storm clouds skittered across the sky, she headed for her bedroom and changed into a pair of jeans and a dark blue T-shirt.

She grabbed a small purse and a backpack, leaving her phone charging on the counter. Stepping from the kitchen into the garage, she hit the lights and stuffed some gloves, a spade, a flashlight, a rope, wire cutters and a few other items into the pack. She opened the garage door and unlocked her truck. The purse went into the front seat and the backpack went into the back.

She returned to the garage and curled one hand around a shovel. She balanced it on her shoulder and approached the truck. The puddle of water in the bed rippled as she laid down the shovel.

Placing her hands on her hips, she pivoted toward the garage and eyed the duffel. She huffed out a breath and strode toward it, her boots clumping on the cement floor of the garage.

She dragged the bag from beneath the counter and hauled it over her shoulder. She swung it onto the floor of the truck's back seat and brushed her hands together—as if that were it. That wasn't it. That was part one.

She climbed into her truck and punched the remote with her knuckle. She watched her garage door settle into place before backing out of her driveway.

When she merged onto the highway, she flicked on her brights. The crescent moon didn't have enough power to light up the desert, and the road didn't have many travelers. When the odd car did approach from the oncoming lane of traffic, she dimmed her lights.

Finally, she didn't meet any other cars coming the other way, and she expelled a breath she didn't even know she'd been holding. Nobody else would be out here at this time of night.

Her headlights illuminated the mile marker on the side of the highway, and she glanced at her odometer to track the miles. At two miles past the marker, she eased off her gas pedal and peered over the steering wheel.

She spotted the break in the highway and turned onto an access road. Her truck bounced and lurched as it ate up the rough ground beneath its wheels.

If you didn't know the fencing was there, you could drive right into it, but she caught the gleam from the metal posts and the heavy-duty wire strung between those posts.

She pulled up next to the fence and cut her lights. Her flashlight would have do. She didn't want to advertise her presence on this land, just in case another driver saw her lights out here from the highway. She hopped from the truck, opened the back door and snagged her backpack first.

Flicking on the flashlight, she ran its beam along

the length of the fence. It hadn't been designed to keep people out so much as to stake a claim.

She ground her teeth together and ducked between the two wires that stretched from post to post. At least nobody had thought to electrify this fence, but again they didn't have anything to protect—not yet.

She stumbled across the desert floor for about twenty feet, and then dropped to her knees at a slight dip. Her flashlight illuminated the area—no rocks, no cactus, no distinguishing features.

She wedged her pack in the dirt to mark the spot and jogged back to her truck. She grabbed the shovel and wrestled the duffel bag from the back seat. The items slowed her progress back to the perfect spot, but she still had enough energy to do what she came here to do.

She dragged the backpack out of the way and plunged her shovel into the sand. In and out, she dipped the shovel into the sand and flicked it out to the side.

Sweating, she pinched her damp T-shirt from her body and surveyed her work. How deep did it have to be? Enough to conceal but not hide forever.

She unzipped the duffel bag at her feet, positioned it at the edge of the hole…and dumped the contents into the shallow grave.

SAM PUSHED HIS laptop away and with it, the faces of the missing people. Gone without a trace. How did that happen? And all of them last seen near the Arizona border towns.

He didn't believe in coincidences.

He'd thought at one point that the bones of the missing might be found in the myriad tunnels that ran between the US and Mexican border, but Border Patrol had gotten a line on most of those tunnels and no bodies had turned up inside them.

Still, the Sonoran Desert provided a vast graveyard. He pulled his laptop toward him again and switched from the faces of the mostly young people to a map of the desert running between Paradiso and the border.

One area on the map jumped out at him, and he traced his fingertip around the red line that marked the location where the new casino was planned. That land, which belonged to the Yaqui tribe, had always been somewhat reachable due to the access road.

He stood up, stretching his arms over his head. He wandered to the window of his motel room and gazed at the drops of water glistening on the glass. The rain had stopped, nothing preventing him from his expedition now.

He grabbed his weapon and his wallet and marched out to his rental car. When did Border

Patrol ever stop working? Especially when an agent didn't have anything better to do.

He pulled out of the motel parking lot and headed toward the highway. His headlights glimmered on the wet asphalt, but on either side of him, the dark desert lurked, keeping its secrets—just like a woman.

Grunting, he hit the steering wheel with the heel of his hand and cranked up the radio. Two days back and the desert had already weaved its spell on him. He'd come to appreciate its mystical, magical aura when he lived here, but the memory had receded when he moved to San Diego. When he left Paradiso, he'd tried to put all those feelings aside—and failed.

When he saw the mile marker winking at him from the side of the road, he grabbed his cell phone and squinted at the directions. He should be seeing the entrance to an access road in about two miles. A few minutes later, he spotted the gap and turned into it, his tires kicking up sand and gravel.

His rental protested by shaking and jerking on the unpaved stretch of road. He gripped the wheel to steady it. "Hold on, baby."

A pair of headlights appeared in the distance, and he blinked his eyes. Did mirages show up at night? Who the hell would be out here?

His heart thumped against his chest. Someone up to no good.

As his car approached the vehicle—a truck by the look of it—he slowed to a crawl. The road couldn't accommodate the two of them passing each other. One of them would have to back into the sand, and a truck, probably with four-wheel drive, could do that a lot better than he could in this midsize with its four cylinders.

The truck jerked to a stop and started backing up at an angle. The driver recognized what Sam had already deduced. The truck would have to be the one to make way but if this dude thought he'd be heading out of here free, clear and anonymous, he didn't realize he'd run headlong into a Border Patrol agent—uniformed or not.

Sam threw his car into Park and left the engine running as he scrambled from the front seat. The driver of the truck revved his engine. Did the guy think he was going to run him over? Take him out in the dead of night?

Sam flipped open his wallet to his ID and badge and rested his other hand on his weapon as he stalked up to the driver's side of the truck.

Holding his badge in front of him and rapping on the hood of the vehicle, he approached the window. "Border Patrol. What's your business out here?"

The window buzzed down, and a pair of luminous dark eyes caught him in their gaze. "Sam? Sam Cross?"

Sam gulped and his heart beat even faster than before as the beam of his flashlight played over the high cheekbones and full lips of the woman he'd loved beyond all reason.

Chapter Two

He growled. "Who is it? Who are you?"

He'd have to try harder than that to sound convincing.

"Oh, please." She shaded her eyes against the intrusive glare of the flashlight. "You know damned well who it is, so get that light out of my face."

He shifted the beam to the side so that it illuminated the ends of her silky ponytail. Bad move. His breath hitched in his throat as he recalled the way that hair had feathered across his bare skin.

"Jolene Nighthawk?"

"In the flesh, Sam." She cut her engine and turned on the dome light in her truck. "What are you doing out here at this time of night?"

"I already asked you that question. It's not safe."

"It's my land...indirectly." She set her jaw, and her nostrils flared. "What could be safer?"

He shoved his hands in his pockets and kicked

sand at her tire. "So, the Yaqui are going ahead with the casino development on the property. Is this your cousin Wade's doing?"

"Wade and the others." She lifted her shoulders. "The tribe put it to a vote, and the Desert Sun Casino won."

"Were you just…surveying the land?" He flung an arm out to the side. "Planting a bomb?"

Jolene jerked her head, her dark eyes flashing. "What does that mean?"

"Just kidding." He held up his hands. "I know you're probably not too happy about the casino. Weren't you trying to prove that any disruption of the land would impact the three-toed tree owl or something?"

She chuckled, and the low sultry sound did something to his insides. "There is no such thing as a three-toed tree owl. I think you mean the elf owl, so points for being close."

He grinned like an idiot, just so damned happy to be in her presence again. "See, I was listening to your lectures."

"Those were supposed to be conversations, not lectures. And no, the environmental study I ordered didn't prove that the casino would disturb the elf owls' habitat, as it's farther west." She gripped the steering wheel with both hands. "In the end, I had nothing."

"That's a good thing, isn't it? I mean, that the

construction site isn't going to impact the desert critters."

"It's not going to affect them as much as it would have to for any alteration in the plans."

"The casino will provide a lot of jobs and generate a lot of money for the tribe, right? I know Border Patrol is involved at some level because some of those new employees will be coming from the Yaqui tribe members in Mexico. The Yaqui governing body has already contacted us." He felt the need to keep talking as Jolene stared at the desert over her steering wheel.

She whipped her head around, her eyes narrowed to slits. "Is that what you're doing out here? Is that why you're in Paradiso?"

Whoa. Had he become the enemy? Who was he kidding? He'd become the enemy the day he'd left her... The day she'd pushed him away.

"I... Something like that." He didn't have to give her all the gory details of his assignment.

She tapped the steering wheel with her long slender fingers. "At this time of night, you're not going to get a very clear picture of the scope of the project, and ground-breaking doesn't start for another two days. The equipment's not even in place yet."

"The rain stopped me from coming out before. I could've put it off until tomorrow, but...it called to me. The desert called to me, and I wanted to see the land before all the hubbub started." Heat rushed from his chest to his face, and he gave thanks to the darkness for its concealment.

"Same." She fired up the truck. "Are you going to be at the ground-breaking ceremony?"

"I'll be there. You?"

"Of course." She threw the truck in Reverse and backed up farther off the access road into the sand. "It's my land."

As she wheeled around him and his rental car, she put her hand out the window and yelled. "Watch out for singing sticks."

Her words caused a chill to run up his spine. She was referring to the Yaqui legend about the boy who killed his brother and buried him in the desert. A small stick with a button on top grew out of the dead boy's head where he was buried. When an old man driving his mules found the stick and grabbed it, the stick sang to him of the boy's death.

The tires of Jolene's truck squealed as they gained purchase on the access road, and Sam watched her taillights until his eyes watered and all he saw was a red blur.

He hopped back into his car and continued on his way. If only all the dead people he was searching for had sticks to mark their burial places.

Two days after his encounter with Jolene, Sam slipped the green shirt of his Border Patrol uniform from its hanger and shook it out. He stuffed his arms in the sleeves and buttoned it to the collar.

It would be hot as blazes at the ground-breaking ceremony for the casino, but he'd be there in an official capacity and couldn't exactly wear shorts and flip-flops. He didn't care. The event would give him another opportunity to see Jolene.

He'd tried to catch sight of her around town, short of stalking her outside her house, but she'd been keeping a low profile. She could've been busy with her duties as a ranger for the National Park Service…but he had a suspicion she was avoiding him.

He didn't blame her, but he'd have liked a chance to tell her his situation now—not that it would make a difference to her. Their meeting the other night showed that she'd clearly moved on.

Looking in the mirror, Sam ran a hand through his hair and then rubbed his front teeth with the pad of his finger—just in case he got to talk with Jolene.

He exited his motel room, and hit the remote for the Border Patrol truck in the parking lot. He climbed inside and made the return trip to the future site of the Yaqui casino.

About thirty minutes later, he slowed down as a line of traffic clogged the highway. Two highway patrol officers were waving people over to the side of the road to park.

Sam rolled down his window and stuck his arm out, flagging down an officer.

A big guy with mirrored sunglasses approached the truck. "You can go around and park at the site. Visitors are parking along the highway and shuttles will take them in to the ground-breaking."

"That's smart. No way all these cars are going to trundle down that road. So, I can pull right in?"

"If you can squeeze through the protestors." The man smirked. "It's a spectacle."

"There are protestors?"

"On the highway. We won't let them go down the access road."

"The Yaqui?" Sam's heartbeat rattled his rib cage.

"Some of them. The ones who don't want the casino. But they've been overruled." The cop rolled his shoulders. "Don't know what they're complaining about. That casino means big money for the tribe and every Yaqui with a card."

"There are more important things than money to some." Sam wheeled around the officer and crawled along the other side of the highway. The infrastructure around here was going to have to change to accommodate the casino. This two-lane highway wouldn't cut it.

As he approached the access road, the decibel level rose and he rolled down his window. Members of the Yaqui tribe were out in force, garbed in native dress, carrying signs, yelling and beating drums. The drums reverberated in Sam's ears, and he held his breath as he peered out the window at the protestors. Would Jolene be one of them?

Sometimes these protests could get unruly and violent, and he didn't want Jolene in the middle of it—not that she would appreciate or even want his protectiveness. He couldn't help it. He couldn't help a lot of things when it came to Jolene Nighthawk. When he didn't see her face among the crowd, he expelled a long breath. Maybe Granny Viv had prevailed upon Jolene to skip the protests today.

He coasted through the divide the highway patrol had forged through the group of protestors. Then he tucked in behind one of the vans ferrying people to the site.

The shuttle turned into a large cleared-out circular area, and Sam followed suit. Colorful flags, that weren't here the other night, drooped in the still air, looking sad instead of festive but that didn't deter the mood of the dignitaries.

A stage had been set up, and Wade Nighthawk, Jolene's cousin, occupied the center of it. He wore his black hair in a sleek ponytail, his only other nod to his Native American heritage, a loose-fitting white shirt embroidered with the animal symbols of the Yaqui, which replaced his usual tailored shirts and suit jacket.

The mayor and other major players clustered on one end of the stage. Sam spotted Nash Dillon talking to a well-dressed older woman. Sam stuck his hand out the window of the truck and pointed at Nash, who nodded back at him. Although Nash was a Border Patrol agent, Nash's family's business had a stake in the casino development, and the dark-haired woman with dramatic gray streaks in her hair was probably involved in the money side of the project.

Clay Archer, the agent in charge of the Paradiso Border Patrol station, gave Sam a thumbs-up from the stage. *Better him than me up there.*

Sam parked and exited his vehicle. He strode up to the stage and clasped hands with Clay.

"Do you have to give a speech or something?"

Clay rolled his eyes. "Just a few words about the Yaqui on the other side of the border and the accommodations we'll make for them to come over and work in the casino."

Nash joined them. "I'd give anything to get off this stage, but my parents insisted I be here and meet the representative for our business group backing the project."

As the woman Nash had been speaking to approached, Sam raised his eyebrow and gave a quick shake of his head.

Nash turned to the woman smoothly. "Karen, I'd like to introduce you to a couple of my fellow Border Patrol agents, Clay Archer and Sam Cross. Sam's out of San Diego. This is Karen Fisher. She's representing the investors."

The attractive woman's smooth face didn't match her graying hair—neither did her strong grip. "Nice to meet you. Thanks for all you do to keep us safe."

Clay, ever the gentleman, said, "Just doing our jobs, ma'am."

Karen drilled Nash with her dark eyes. "What are you doing here from…?"

"San Diego."

"That's right. I suppose you have even more problems with drugs coming across the border there, don't you?"

"We do."

"Sam, welcome back." Wade leaned past the others, extending his hand, his white teeth blinding against his brown skin.

The guy had the smile of a politician. Sam pumped his hand. "Good to see you, Wade. Congratulations."

"Thank you. This is going to mean a lot for Paradiso, as well as the tribe. But then—" Wade cocked his head and his ponytail slid over his shoulder "—you don't live here anymore, so it won't mean much to you. Granny told me you were in town, though. Business?"

"Uh-huh." Sam shifted his gaze to the right and left of the stage.

"Doesn't mean you can't combine a little pleasure with the business." Wade winked. "Jolene's by the equipment to the right."

Before Sam could deny he was searching for Jolene, Wade stepped back and slapped the back of Mayor Zamora. Total politician.

"I'm going to head over there." Sam tipped his head in the general direction of the heavy equipment ready to gouge the earth.

Clay raised his eyebrows. "You do that. I'm gonna practice my speech."

"We should probably take our seats." Nash cupped Karen's elbow and she nodded in Sam's direction.

Sam wended his way through the crowd of people, his step picking up when he saw Jolene helping Granny Viv into a seat. Granny Viv could be his excuse, not that he didn't want to see the old lady anyway. He'd been a favorite of hers— until he'd broken her granddaughter's heart.

He licked his lips as he walked up to the women, his tongue sweeping up grains of sand.

He squeezed Granny Viv's shoulder. "Finally, I get to see my favorite person in Paradiso."

Granny Viv cranked her head to the side. "You

sound like Wade now. Nothing stopping you from dropping in at the rez for a visit."

"Been busy with work." Sam gave the old woman a hug. "You don't look a day older since I left."

"You *are* just like Wade." She wagged a gnarled finger at him. "Are you just going to ignore him, Jolene?"

"Gran, sit." She patted the back of the chair where she'd placed a cushion for her grandmother. "Hello, Sam. How are you?"

Oh, they were playing it like that—like they hadn't run into each other in the middle of the night at this very place the night before last. Two could play that game.

He wrapped his arms around her and pulled her in for a hug. Her soft body yielded to his for a second before she stiffened in his arms.

"Good to see you, Jolene. I was glad I didn't spy you out front with the protestors—for safety's sake."

She reared back from him until he dropped his arms. "Protest is futile. Clay giving a speech up there?"

That hug had affected him more than it had her, and his tight throat made it hard to speak. "Something about the Yaqui on the other side of the border."

Granny Viv patted the chair next to her. "Sit here for the festivities."

Jolene gripped the back of the chair. "I thought I was sitting next to you, Gran?"

"I see you all the time. Let Sam sit here, and you can sit on the other side of him."

Sam plopped down in the seat to claim it before Jolene could, as if playing a game of musical chairs. "No place else I'd rather be."

With no other choice, Jolene sat next to him, crossing one long leg over the other, her eyebrows creating a V over her nose.

Mayor Zamora stepped up to the mic and tapped it. "Everyone enjoying the food and the dancers?"

He paused for the scattered applause and launched into his speech about the importance of the Yaqui tribe to the area and its cultural contributions.

The mayor's words flowed over Sam, one running into the other. Sam's attention was fully focused on Jolene's leg kicking back and forth. She usually favored jeans and boots, but today a light skirt rippled around her calves and each time she kicked out her foot, the slit in the skirt parted to reveal the smooth skin of her thigh.

Her elbow jabbed his shoulder. "Are you even paying attention?"

"What? Yeah, cultural contributions." He adjusted his sunglasses and peered at the stage where the flags had started flapping.

"I said, I wasn't sure how a gambling casino was a Yaqui cultural asset. They'll probably decorate it with our icons—ugh." Her full lips flattened into a snarl.

"Shh." Granny Viv reached across Sam and poked Jolene's arm. "Your cousin's up next."

Wade took the mayor's place at the mic and gave a loud whoop. The crowd went nuts and answered him in kind.

Jolene rolled her eyes and pointed at the darkening sky. "Looks like it's going to rain on their parade."

The wind had picked up and the once-pathetic flags snapped in the breeze, clapping along with the audience. Wade knew how to work a crowd, for sure. Little eddies of sand swirled on the desert floor, a sure sign of the oncoming monsoon.

He tilted his head toward hers. "Maybe they'll get through all the pomp and circumstance, and the mayor and Wade can toss a shovelful of sand over their shoulders before the big machines get to work."

"Will the excavators still work in the rain?" She folded her hands over her knee, twisting her fingers.

"Sure. After all this, they'll want to get started on the big dig."

Her restless hands moved to her skirt where she pleated the material, released it and pleated it again.

Jolene might've been happier out there with the protestors, but after the death of Jolene's father, Wade took the reins of the Nighthawk family and the family members had always been part of the Yaqui governing board. Bad optics for one Nighthawk cousin to be in here cheerleading the casino and the other out there carrying signs.

Clay did his part up there, and then the speeches ended. Both Mayor Zamora and Wade raised their ceremonial shovels and stepped from the stage. Someone came forward with wire cutters and snipped the wires between the posts, creating an opening for the two dignitaries.

They both plunged their shovels into the sand at the same time, as a cheer rose from the crowd and the cameras came out.

Jolene sat stiffly beside him, barely taking a breath.

Sam touched her shoulder. "Did you get anything to eat? Do you want something from one of the food trucks?"

She flashed a smile at him that nearly knocked him off his chair. "Yeah, that would be great."

He hadn't expected that response. He figured she'd want to hightail it out of here as fast as she could. He asked Granny Viv if she wanted something to eat and she sent him and Jolene off in quest of some chili.

As they sauntered toward the food trucks, Jolene took a deep breath. "That rain is coming, but I think they'll be able to start digging before the deluge, don't you?"

"All of a sudden, you seem anxious for them to get to work." He shot her a glance from the side of his eye.

"It's like a bandage. Peel it off all at once." She jerked her thumb toward a food truck to the right. "I think this one has the chili Gran wants."

They shuffled in line until they reached the window, and Sam ordered three cups of chili and some bottles of water. He grabbed a straw when he picked up the food, and on their way back to Gran, he and Jolene squeezed their way through the people gawking at the excavators gulping up the sand and spitting it out in big piles.

When they reached Granny Viv, Sam placed the chili in her hands and put the bottle of water with the straw sticking out of it on the empty chair next to her. "Watch out. It's hot."

A clap of thunder boomed in the distance as if to emphasize his precaution.

The chatter level seemed to rise with the echoes of the thunder, and a mass of people began to surge toward the build site, knocking over a few chairs in the process.

"What's going on?" Jolene poked him in the back. "You're tall. Can you see what's happening? Something other than the thunder got all these people excited."

"I'm not sure." Sam peered above the bobbing heads. "A couple of the workmen are shouting and running toward the stage."

"I hope nobody's hurt." Granny Viv held her spoon full of steaming chili suspended in the air, halfway to her mouth.

Sam placed his food next to the water on the chair. "I'll check it out."

"I'm coming with you." Jolene added her bowl to the collection on the chair and hooked a finger in his belt loop. "Lead the way."

If she were willing to follow him, he'd lead her wherever she wanted to go.

Sam plowed through the clutches of people, with Jolene right behind him. When he reached the stage, he grabbed Clay's arm. "What's going on, Clay?"

"Not sure." He nodded toward the piles of sand and dirt. "The work crew found something, I think."

Sam edged closer to a couple of guys throwing their arms around and talking a mile a minute.

One shouted in Wade's face. "We have to stop. We have to stop."

A flush rose to Wade's cheeks. "Don't be ridiculous. It's nothing. Keep going."

The driver of one of the excavators dug his work boots into the sand. "I won't. I won't continue."

The other worker crossed himself and said, *"Dios mio."*

Jolene called out, her voice rising above the din. "Wade, what's wrong? What is it?"

Wade's head whipped around, a scowl marring his smooth face. "It's nothing. Nonsense."

The mayor shook his head. "Well, I'll be damned. Seems like the boys dug up some bones. We might've just stumbled on a graveyard."

Chapter Three

Jolene folded her arms across her midsection. "Bones? Human bones?"

"That's just it, Jolene, it could be anything, one of those extinct animals you care so much about." Wade flicked his long fingers toward the two workmen. "Do these guys look like archaeologists to you?"

"Are you?" She slashed a hand through the air, figuratively trying to wipe the smirk from Wade's face. "Watch your tone. They know what they saw."

Sam whistled through his teeth and murmured in her ear. "That's going to put a crimp in old Wade's plans, isn't it?"

She whispered. "He's right. Those bones could belong to anything."

"Or anyone." Sam's jaw tensed. "Didn't the mayor mention a graveyard? More than one set of bones?"

"Whatever it was, it shook up the crew." Jolene

put a hand on Sam's back as he made a quick turn. "Where are you going?"

"I figure Clay and I know a human bone when we see one." He waved his arm in the air at Clay. "Hey, Clay!"

Clay joined them. "Did you hear that? They dug up some bones?"

"Are you thinking what I'm thinking? Let's go have a look. It doesn't seem like anyone else wants to investigate." He squeezed Jolene's shoulder. "Wait here."

"No way." She strode after the two Border Patrol agents. "You don't think I know animal bones when I see them? Ruling out is as important as identifying."

Sam cranked his head over his shoulder. "I know better than to try to stop you from doing anything."

He couldn't stop her from loving him, either. But then, he hadn't tried that hard.

The three of them trudged through the sand toward the heavy equipment, its jaws suspended in the air, wide open and frozen. They stopped at the edge of a hole in the ground and peered down into it.

Clay jabbed a finger toward the sand. "There. It's a long bone. Looks like a femur."

"Could be a coyote, a sheep." Sam slapped at

a big drop of rain that had fallen on the side of his neck.

Jolene's gaze darted between the bones in the pit, and then she twisted her head over her shoulder and surveyed the ground to the side of the excavator. A smooth crescent protruded from the sand.

She broke away from Clay and Sam and wandered toward the pile of dirt the excavator had dumped after a few digs. Crouching down, she brushed the sand away from the white dome and called over her shoulder. "You think this is from a coyote, too?"

Both men strode toward her and peeked over her shoulder at the human skull next to the wheel of the excavator.

Clay got on his phone. "I'm calling Paradiso PD. They should have a car out here anyway, monitoring those protestors."

"I'll give Wade and Mayor Zamora the bad news. This construction has to stop now. This could be a crime scene." Sam pivoted in the sand and scuffed toward the stage.

Jolene's heart pounded, and she tugged on the back of his shirt. "Crime scene? What do you mean a crime scene?"

"Those bones could belong to a murder victim." His eyebrows snapped over his nose.

"You're the one who found the skull. You know it doesn't belong to an animal."

"A murder victim?" She swiveled her head around, taking in the swirl of activity—the colors, the voices, the smells—and tilted to the side.

Sam grabbed her around the waist. "What's wrong? Are you feeling faint? Did the bones upset you?"

"The crush of people is getting to me. I'm going to collect Gran and get out of here." As she whirled away from Sam, Wade stormed up to her and pinched her upper arm between his thumb and forefinger. "What did you do?"

She yanked out of her cousin's grasp and stumbled into Sam. "Me? I didn't do anything."

"You were out there. I heard you found the human skull." He jabbed a finger into her chest. "Why do you have to go nosing into everything? I could've handled the guys. We could've…"

"What, Wade? Swept it under the rug? Kept it hidden?"

Sam had been on the phone during her exchange with Wade and when her cousin had gotten up close and personal, Sam swung around and smoothly stepped between them. "Whoa, Wade. You need to calm down. There was no hiding those bones. Do you think if Jolene hadn't discovered the skull, Clay and I wouldn't have seen it? The gruesome discovery shook up those work-men. They never would've kept quiet."

Wade stretched his lips, his plastic smile melt-ing into a sneer. "You have no idea the effect a few bucks can have on a man's nerves."

"I wouldn't be spouting off about your brib-ery skills if I were you, Wade." Sam held up his phone. "I called the Paradiso PD, and they're sending a car back. They're gonna put yellow crime scene tape up to replace your multicolored ribbons. Then the Pima County Sheriff's Depart-ment is going to send their CSIs out here to col-lect those bones."

Jolene swallowed. "What are they going to do with the bones?"

"Test them, measure them, analyze them. Maybe discover the identity of the person." Sam smacked Wade on the back. "Don't look so bummed, Wade. Once they clear out those bones and check the area for more, your project should be able to get back on track—in a year."

"This isn't going to deter us." Wade smoothed a hand over his face, putting his calm, unruf-fled facade back in place. "You should take Gran home, Jolene."

"That's what I was just going to do." A fat rain-drop splashed on the back of her hand. "And not a minute too soon."

"I'll come with you." Sam cupped her elbow

and guided her through the thinning crowd. "Wade's a piece of work."

"He's a piece of something." She shook him off. "You don't have to protect me against Wade—or anything else."

She'd been getting too comfortable with Sam's little gestures—the touches, the consideration, the fawning over Gran—scratch that last one. Gran adored Sam and reveled in the attentions he gave her.

When they got back to the chairs where they'd left Gran, two teens were sprawled across them, their noses buried in their phones.

Jolene recognized one of them. "Andrew, did you see my grandmother here?"

He lifted one eyebrow without raising his gaze from his phone. "Yeah, she left with my grandmother. They told me to stay here and let you know when you got back—and they took your car."

"They took my car?" Jolene peered at the sky. "Why'd they do that?"

Andrew shrugged one shoulder. "Me and my friend wanted to stay, so Granny Viv told my grandma to take your keys and your car so they could leave. I can drive you."

Jolene snagged her purse from under the chair. "That's okay, Andrew. I'll get a ride…"

"With me." Sam looked down his nose at the boy. "You're old enough to drive?"

"Got my license and everything." He socked his friend in the arm. "Let's go see if we can get a look at those bones."

As the boys slouched off, Sam turned to Jolene. "Do you mind waiting until I talk to the Paradiso PD? They'll probably want to talk to you, too."

"Me?" Her voice squeaked and she cleared her throat. "Why would they want to talk to me?"

"You found the skull."

"I didn't find it. The skull was lying on the ground." She adjusted her purse over her shoulder and folded her arms. The less she was involved with this, the better.

"It wasn't lying on the ground. Clay and I wouldn't have missed it if it were." He placed a hand on her back. "They're here."

Jolene glanced up at the officers talking to Wade and the two workmen. Wade had recovered his equilibrium and had the appearance of complete cooperation with the work stoppage. His wife, Cerisse, would get a whole different perspective at home tonight.

Sam greeted the cops and told them how he and Clay had gone out to look at the bones, just to see if they were human. He jerked his thumb toward her. "And the minute Jolene found the skull, we knew what we had."

The officer didn't have many questions for them and Jolene convinced Sam to leave before the sheriffs came on the scene.

"We left our names with the officer. If the sheriff's deputies want to contact us, they can." She tipped her head back to take in the darkening sky. "Besides, we're going to be caught in the deluge in a few minutes."

"At least we don't have to wait for the shuttle." He pointed out a Border Patrol vehicle parked behind the food trucks. "I got preferred parking."

As he opened the door of the truck for her, the rain started coming down in earnest. She ducked in quickly, and he slammed the door.

By the time he slid behind the wheel, his shirt was already soaked.

"It's going to be another monsoon like the other day."

"It is the season for them. How was the summer? Any rain then?"

"Not much. Looks like the clouds are making up for the dry months."

Sam followed one of the shuttle vans down the access road and swerved around it when they hit the highway.

He gestured toward the phone cupped in her hands. "Do you want to call Rosie and see if she and your grandmother made it home okay?"

"I'll give them more time to get there. I don't

want to distract Rosie if she's driving. It's bad enough that her grandson Andrew is out here on the road."

"You didn't tell Granny Viv that we ran into each other the night before last." He slid a glance her way, and then concentrated on the road.

"I didn't want to worry her."

"Because she knows how upset you are about the casino going in?"

"Oh, I'm not that upset." She smoothed her hands over her skirt. "Progress, right? Wade told me how many jobs the casino will bring to the area…and our people. That can't be a bad thing. I understand Nash Dillon is involved in the project."

"Yeah." Sam rubbed his chin. "I think he's more involved with his job with the Border Patrol than he is with his family's business, but he was at the ground-breaking with the rep for one of the big financial backers."

"His family has that silent partner—the one who invested in the pecan-processing plant with them. I think he has a financial stake in the casino."

"Not him, personally. It's that Karen… Fisher who's repping the consortium. Nash has his hands full with the baby he and his fiancée are adopting."

"Yeah, Nash with a baby." She stared out the

window at the rivulets of water squiggling down the glass—just like tears. She should ask him about his own child, his daughter. Her throat tightened, and she rested her forehead against the window.

"My wife and I are divorced." He blurted out the words, and they hung in the car between them.

Should she pick them up or let them settle and dissolve?

"I heard that one before." She put a hand over her mouth to stop any more accusations from flying out.

"Jolene, I never told you I was divorced." The truck hit a puddle and water splashed the window causing her to jerk back.

"Separated, divorced. You told me they were the same thing." She held her left hand out to the side, palm out. "I know. I believed what I wanted to believe."

"I thought my marriage was over, Jolene. I wanted it to be over. I wanted to be with you." He slammed a fist against the dashboard.

Her fingers plucked at the material of her skirt. "I know you had to choose your daughter over me. I understand. Neither of us would've been happy if you'd abandoned your baby."

"And yet, here I am." He cranked on the defroster as the windows started fogging over.

"Working out of state, my daughter in San Diego. Babies can't save failing marriages."

"You had to try." Her eyes followed the slapping windshield wipers, their motion almost hypnotizing her. "Wh-what's her name?"

"Jessica. I call her Jess." His fingers flexed on the steering wheel, and his tight jaw relaxed. "She just turned two."

Jolene knew exactly how old Sam's child was. It had been over two years now since he'd left her and broken her heart. She could've stopped him. He'd been waiting for her to stop him, but he would've hated himself and eventually he'd have hated her, too.

His own father had abandoned Sam, his brother and mother when Sam was just three years old. He could never do that to a child of his own.

Whatever had happened between him and his wife when he went back to the marriage must've been intolerable for him to end it.

She swiped a hand beneath her nose. "Is Jess talking?"

"Nonstop words and babble." He made the turn onto her street.

"Do you want to come in for a little while? There's someone who'd like to see you."

"Chip? You still have Chip?"

"Of course." She wouldn't tell him she'd soaked

Chip's fur with her tears every night after Sam had left. Only she and Chip ever had to know that.

He pulled into her driveway, and she hopped out of the truck before he cut the engine. She ran to her covered walkway, holding her purse over her head to deflect the rain.

She stopped halfway to the door and cocked her head. "Do you hear that?"

"Sounds like a wild bear trying to claw his way outside."

"Chip knows you're here. He never gets that excited when I come home." She nudged a flowerpot to the side and stooped down to pick up her house key. As she pounded on the door with the heel of her hand, she said, "You'd better settle down in there. You should be on your best behavior."

She cracked the door open and Chip thrust his wet nose into the opening. "Are you ready, Sam?"

"Bring it on." Sam crouched down, bracing himself.

When Jolene swung open the door, Chip hurtled himself toward Sam and nearly bowled him over. Wagging his tail, Chip put his front paws on Sam's chest and bathed his face in dog kisses.

"Look at you." Sam hung his arm around the dog's neck and patted his side. "He's so big now. Is he a good guard dog?"

"The best. Can't you tell by the greeting he

gave you?" She tugged on Chip's collar. "C'mon, you silly boy."

She widened the door, but Chip wouldn't budge until Sam rose and strode over the threshold.

Shutting the door behind them, she placed the extra key on the table in the entryway and hung up her wet purse on the peg next to the umbrella she could've used earlier. "Do you want something to drink?"

"Just water." He pulled the shirt of his uniform out of the waistband of his pants. "You know what I'd really like?"

Her heart fluttered and her mouth got dry as she watched Sam's fingers undo the top button on his shirt. She couldn't go there with him again, no matter how desperately her body yearned for his touch.

He raised an eyebrow. "If it's not too much trouble, I'd like to borrow your dryer for about twenty minutes before I go back to the station. This wet shirt is really uncomfortable."

"Of course, yes." She ducked down to pet Chip, letting her hair shield her warm face.

"The T-shirt, too?"

She glanced up at Sam, his shirt gaping open over a white V-neck T-shirt.

"I'm soaked to the skin."

"No problem." She scratched Chip behind one floppy ear. "I don't have anything you can wear unless you want to put on a robe. It's black but it does have flowers on it. I won't take pictures, I swear."

"It's not exactly cold, is it? I'll pass—not that I don't trust you."

She flicked her hair over her shoulder. What did he mean by that?

He shrugged out of his shirt and yanked at the hem of his T-shirt, peeling the wet cotton from his torso.

With the T-shirt over Sam's head, Jolene drank in the sight of his lean, muscled body. Her fingertips tingled with the memory of his smooth, warm flesh and the need ached in her gut.

He pulled the shirt off his head, and she turned toward the kitchen. "I'll get you that water and stuff those things in the dryer for you—as long as you don't expect me to iron anything."

"Lucky for both of us, the uniform doesn't need ironing." He followed her into the kitchen, holding his damp shirts in his hands in front of him, like an offering, facing her across the small center island.

"You can put those on the counter." She nodded toward the island as she reached for the cupboard and grabbed a glass. "We never got to finish our chili, did we? Are you hungry?"

"I'll pick up something on my way back to

the station." He perched on a stool, only his bare chest visible above the edge of the counter.

If anyone had told her this morning she'd have Sam Cross half-naked in her kitchen by the afternoon, she'd have…thanked them.

She filled the glass with ice and water from her fridge and set it before him with a tap on the counter. Wiggling her fingers, she said, "Why are you still holding those wet things? Give them to me."

"Didn't want to get your gleaming counter all wet." He held out the bundle of clothes to the side, and she circled the island to take them, her gaze avoiding all that bare male flesh in front of her.

She took the shirts with both hands and walked back through the kitchen to the laundry room. "Perfect timing. I have some things in the wash that need to go in the dryer. We can save on electricity."

"I don't want my shirt to get your stuff dirty."

"It's fine. It's just a few towels and…other things." She tossed Sam's shirts in the dryer and then piled her own clothes in after. She plucked a dryer sheet from the box and threw it in with the rest. She jabbed a few buttons, took a deep breath and returned to the kitchen.

"You never told me what you were doing in Paradiso? Some case you're working?"

"Yeah, a case." He ran the side of his thumb

down the sweating glass. "And that's why I want to thank you, Jolene."

"Thank me?" She poked a finger into her chest. "For what? How did I help your case?"

Sam gulped back the rest of the water and smacked the glass on the counter. "By planting those bones at the construction site."

Chapter Four

Sam narrowed his eyes, as he watched a rosy flush creep up Jolene's face. She'd just confirmed his suspicions.

"You think I planted those bones at the construction site? That's what you think I was doing there the other night?" Her long lashes fluttered with every blink of her eyes. "Wh-why would I do that?"

"C'mon, Jolene. What do you take me for?" He crossed his arms over his chest, probably losing a little of the high ground without his shirt. "You're out there in the middle of the night, a shovel in the bed of your pickup and a set of bones appears on the day of the ground-breaking for a casino you detest."

"That's crazy." She swept his glass from the counter and spun toward the sink. "Where would I get bones, anyway?"

"You're a resourceful woman. I'm sure it didn't take you long to figure out how to get your hands on a set of bones. And—" he leveled a finger at her "—you made sure we found the skull, because you knew it was there."

Pulling back her shoulders, she tilted up her chin. "You can't prove anything."

"Give me a month or two, and I'm sure I could prove it." He rested his arms on the counter and hunched his shoulders. "But I'm not interested in nailing you for planting bones. I'm not sure that's even a crime."

"Why not? Why even bring it up if you don't care?" She set the glass in the sink and turned, gripping the edge of the counter behind her.

"I didn't say I didn't care. Didn't I thank you for doing it?"

"You're not making any sense. I'm not admitting to anything, but why should you be happy if *someone* left bones there?"

"Because that helps my case." He scratched his jaw. "Can I have some more water, please? All this explaining is making me thirsty."

"That's funny. I don't hear you explaining much of anything. You're throwing around accusations and talking about some case. You still haven't told me why you're here." She snatched up his glass from the sink, and his leftover ice tinkled as she filled it again.

"Missing people."

Her hand jerked as she set the glass down, and the water sloshed over the side. "Missing people?"

Drawing an invisible line on the counter with this finger, he said, "There was a cluster of missing people southeast of San Diego at about the same time we saw an influx of a particularly pure form of meth, pink meth. We saw a similar pattern here in Paradiso from a few years ago. As I'd worked in this area before, my commander sent me here to look into it."

"I don't get it." She dabbled her fingers in the puddle of water on the counter. "People go missing all the time. Why do these folks warrant closer scrutiny than all the other missing people?"

He formed a circle with both of his hands. "This is a cluster. It's a higher than average number of people who have gone missing. They all disappeared close to the border—here and in San Diego—and they vanished at a time when we started seeing this new meth on the street."

"How is the discovery of bones in the desert going to help your investigation?"

Sam rubbed his chin. "On the border in California, out in the desert, we found a graveyard of bones. We're still identifying them, but so far they belong to the people who disappeared at the same time the pink meth showed up. It makes me think there's a similar graveyard out here, and I want a chance to do some digging, literally, before that casino comes in and covers it all up."

"What makes you think it's in that location?" Jolene hugged herself and rubbed her arms.

He'd gladly hold her in his arms to do the hugging, but even though she'd been the one who had insisted he return to his pregnant wife, she hadn't forgiven him for leaving…yet. He swallowed. "A tip I received."

"You're not going to tell me what it was?"

"I'd rather not, but now I can use the discovery of the bones you dumped there to turn this into more than a wild goose chase. Question." He shoved his glass toward her and splayed his hands on the countertop. "What's your plan once the experts figure out the bones you buried don't belong to some ancient member of the Yaqui tribe? That the land is not a sacred Yaqui burial site?"

Her full lips parted, and her lashes swept over her eyes. Then she squared her shoulders and tossed her hair over her shoulder. "I hadn't thought that far ahead. My goal was to halt the immediate ground-breaking—and I did."

Progress. Sam eased out a breath. He'd had no proof that Jolene had planted the bones at the construction site, so the fact that she'd admitted it to him signaled a thaw in the icy chill she'd maintained since seeing him again.

"That you did." He winked at her. "I'm not

going to ask you where you got them because I know you have friends in high places…or at least academic places, but how'd you know the exact place to put them? They could've started digging anywhere."

A small smile twisted her lips. "I have a map of the construction site, which includes phases, including where the first hole was going. It's all very specific."

"Let me guess." He ran a hand over his chest, and Jolene's gaze followed the movement like a feather across his skin. It made him hard. If just a look from her luminous dark eyes could do that to him, he was in more trouble than he'd expected coming back here.

"Yes? What's your guess?" She quirked an eyebrow at him.

"Umm…" he shook his head "…that you got it from your cousin somehow."

"I did. Gran is always using Wade's phone. I took a peek at it, saw the plans and printed them out from his phone. I hadn't formulated my scheme yet, but seeing those plans gave me a few ideas." She snapped her fingers. "And it worked."

"For now. It's not going to take forensics long to figure out those bones are not part of a Yaqui graveyard, especially with Wade and his backers pushing for results." He nudged a sleeping Chip with the toe of his boot, and the dog thumped his tail once.

"Nash Dillon? Do you think Nash will be pushing him?" She wrapped a lock of hair around her finger. "Do you think Nash can do anything to stop the casino? Would he?"

"I don't know if he would or not. Most people around here think the casino is a good idea, Jolene."

"Most people don't have a father who was murdered out there." Her bottom lip quivered, and Sam pushed up from the stool.

He skirted the counter and cupped her face with one hand. "I know. I'm sorry, and I'm sorry nobody was ever brought to justice for that crime. Is that the reason you're against the casino?"

"If Joe Blackhawk were alive today, there would be no question of a casino going on that land." She cinched his wrist with her fingers. "Don't you see, Sam? The two events are linked. My father was murdered to clear the way for the casino."

"What are you saying? You think Wade killed your father?"

"I don't know." She released his arm, made a half turn and braced her hands against the counter. "It's like your missing people. It's just too much of a coincidence."

He reached out to touch her back, and then

pulled away at the sound of the buzzer on the dryer. "The authorities put your father's murder down to the drug trade—he saw something or someone he shouldn't have seen out there."

"I know what they say." She straightened up and squeezed past him, her filmy blouse brushing against the bare skin of his chest. "I just don't believe it."

He watched the sway of her hips in the floral skirt as she walked away from him, and he squeezed his eyes closed. What would Jolene think of him if she knew he was consumed by visions of her in his bed while she was talking to him about her father?

"I don't think you're going to have much luck with Nash. His family business is part of some consortium that makes investment decisions over which he has little to no control. He just sits back and reaps the profits."

She floated back into the kitchen with his shirts draped over her arm. "It was just an idea. Nash has always been so easygoing—and I know his fiancée's father was also killed, in the line of duty. I thought she might be sympathetic."

"I'm sure she would be. I'm sure they both would be, but like I said, Nash is carried along with the business with little control over the decisions. His parents set it up that way, as neither

Nash nor his sister had much interest in the day-to-day running of the corporation."

She dangled his shirts from her fingertips. "All dry."

As he swept them from her grasp, a pair of black lacy panties loosened from his T-shirt and drifted to the floor. He plucked them up between two fingers and waved them in the air. "Damn, busted. I didn't think I'd taken these off, too."

She snatched them back from him and crumpled the silky material in her fist. "Very funny. I told you I put your things in with my laundry."

Chuckling, he pulled the warm T-shirt over his head. As he poked his head out of the neck, he said, "I think I can help you with the second part of your plan."

"You're going to use the discovery of the bones to launch an investigation into that construction area as a possible burial site for those missing people."

"Exactly." He shook out his uniform shirt and hung it on the back of a kitchen chair. "It won't carry the same weight as a sacred site, but it will definitely cause delays in the construction."

"Does that mean you're not going to tell anyone that I dropped those bones there?" She swept her tongue along her bottom lip.

"Why should I? The interruption you caused will give me some time to poke around that land.

Then when forensics discovers the bones are...
whatever they are, I'll have another reason to halt
the project. Maybe I'll make a similar discovery
in Paradiso as we did south of San Diego." He put
his finger to his lips. "And you won't tell anyone
about my plans, either, right?"

"My lips are sealed."

He stuck out his hand. "Then we have a deal."

"Deal." She curled her hand around his, her
smooth flesh sending tingles up his arm.

She started to pull away, but he held fast, running the pad of his thumb across the back of her
hand. "How have you been, otherwise? You look
good."

She left her hand in his. "I'm fine. I still enjoy
my work. The extended family is doing well.
Chip's my constant companion."

He'd already asked around about Jolene's marital and dating status, and he'd been relieved to
find out she was single and not dating anyone
special. He squeezed her hand before releasing
it. "Happy?"

"Outside of the garbage going on with the casino? Yeah, happy. And you? What happened to
your marriage?"

He shrugged. "What didn't happen? I knew it
was doomed the minute I moved back there...or
at least after the birth of Jess."

"Aimee didn't change after Jess was born?" Jolene placed a hand against her heart.

"Nope—still the life of every party."

"Is she still using?" Her fingers curled against her blouse. "Not while she was pregnant?"

"She stopped at first, but I think she was taking drugs at the end." He slammed a fist on the counter. "I should've seen it, but she hid it from me. Lied."

"And Jess?" Jolene's eyes widened. "Is she okay?"

"She was premature and low birth weight. She's been a little slow with certain milestones. That's when I knew for sure Aimee had been using, even though she still denied it. She made a show of attending NA meetings, but that all fell apart when I followed her once and caught her in some guy's car smoking meth after the meeting."

"Oh, my God, Sam. I didn't realize it was so bad. What about Jess now? Is she with Aimee?"

"Aimee's mother is staying at the house while I'm gone. Aimee dumps Jess on her mom most of the time it's her turn to have her, anyway. I can trust Aimee's mom. Jess is in good hands."

"That must be so hard on you, Sam. So hard for Jess." She touched his shoulder. "I'm sorry."

He flinched. He didn't want Jolene back because she felt sorry for him.

"It's my fault. I should've known what I was

getting into when I married Aimee, but then I was her partner in crime in those days."

"But you changed. You gave up the drinking. You grew up, and she didn't." Jolene tucked her hair behind one ear. "Do you think you could ever get full custody of Jess? Is that something you'd want to do?"

"I've started looking into it. We've been separated over a year, and the divorce was finalized a few months ago." He held up two fingers. "I swear."

"I believe you." She dipped her head once. "Maybe you could give me a ride to Gran's house, so I can pick up my car. I don't know what she was thinking taking off like that."

"I hope she wasn't feeling ill." Sam flicked his shirt off the chair, not unhappy with the abrupt change of subject, and punched an arm through one sleeve. Granny Viv was most likely scheming to get him and Jolene back together. She was always solidly rooting for the two of them—until he'd betrayed Jolene by lying about the last time he and Aimee had slept together.

He hadn't thought that detail would matter. He'd been trying to make himself more marketable to Jolene by distancing himself from his marriage. He never dreamed Aimee would get pregnant, especially as she'd assured him she'd been on the pill during her recovery.

That had been one of the hardest things he'd had to do in his life—tell Jolene that the wife he was separated from, the wife he supposedly hadn't been intimate with since their separation six months before, was three months pregnant with his baby.

He smoothed his shirt over his chest and buttoned it up. "Do you mind if I have a look at that map?"

"If you think what you're doing can delay the project, then of course. I can make a copy of it for you on my printer, or you can take a picture of it with your phone." She held up her finger. "It's in my office."

She crossed the living room to an open door near the front entrance where she'd set up a small office. She called out. "It's just an eight-and-a-half-by-eleven sheet of paper, but it's detailed. Showed me where the first dig was going to be, anyway."

As Sam tucked in his shirt, he heard banging and rustling from the office. Maybe Jolene was making him a copy.

He buckled his equipment belt around his waist and strode to the office door. Poking his head inside, he said, "Are you making that copy?"

Jolene spun around, gripping her empty hands in front of her, her eyes dark pools. "It's gone, Sam. Somebody came in here and stole that map."

Chapter Five

Jolene dropped to her knees and rested the side of her face on the cool floor as she reached out with one hand to feel beneath the desk. "Maybe it fell to the floor."

Her words sounded hollow to her own ears. It hadn't fallen to the floor. She'd left it in the top right drawer of her desk.

Sam walked into the room, his boots clomping on the tile. He loomed over her. "Where did you have it?"

She sat up, bumping her head on the underside of the desk. "I put it in the drawer."

"Is the drawer full? Could it have gotten stuck?" He yanked open the drawer, and a couple of pens rattled. He shuffled through the sticky notepads, a few business cards and some slips of paper with usernames and passwords scribbled across them.

"It's gone, Sam." She sat cross-legged on the floor, rubbing the side of her head. "Someone broke into my house and took it."

"Is your head okay?" He extended his hand to her, and she grabbed it, more to steady her nerves than for assistance getting up.

"The head's fine. I'm not." She swept her hands across the neat desk. "Who would want that map? Why wouldn't he or she want me to have it?"

"And how'd this person even know you had the map?" Sam leaned his thigh against the desk. "Obviously, someone didn't randomly break into your house, see a map in a drawer and steal it on a whim, unless…"

"Unless what?" She pressed a hand against her stomach, trying to still the butterflies there— and this time they had nothing to do with Sam's touch.

"Is there anything else missing?"

She twisted her head from side to side. "Not that I noticed."

"When was the last time you consulted the map? If you looked at it this morning, the theft occurred when you were at the ground-breaking." He tapped a knuckle against the desk. "Did you happen to take a picture of it with your phone?"

"I should have, but I didn't." She balled her hand into a fist. "I haven't seen the map since the night I dumped the bones at the construction site. I had it with me that night."

"Could you have lost it there? Left it in your car?"

"I wish." The corner of her eye twitched. "I had it in my backpack when I went out there. When I came home, I unloaded my pack and put the map back in the drawer. I'm sure of it."

"So, somebody broke in at some point after that night." He swept his arm out to the side. "Have a look around. See if anything else is gone. Maybe it was just a common thief burglarizing your place, saw the map and thought it was buried treasure or something."

"Really?" She put a hand on her hip. "X marks the spot?"

He flicked a finger beneath her chin. "I'm exaggerating. Maybe he thought he could use it to blackmail someone. Look around."

"Computer's still here." She tapped the top of her closed laptop. "Printer."

She yanked open the top drawer of a two-drawer oak filing cabinet and thumbed through some files. "My passport, birth certificate, social security card, all here."

"Forget that stuff. What about valuables? Money? Jewelry?"

"Jewelry? You know I don't own any expensive pieces of jewelry." She held her arm in front of her and jangled the wooden bangles on her wrist. "I do have a safe with some cash and a few weapons."

Sam's head jerked up. "Weapons?"

"A couple of pieces my dad left me. If he'd have had one of them the night he was murdered, he'd probably still be here." Her eyes stung as she spun away from Sam. "The safe's in my bedroom closet."

He closed the desk drawer and followed her out of the office.

When she walked into her bedroom, she made a beeline for the walk-in closet and flicked on the switch on the wall outside. She pulled open the door, shoved aside some blouses hanging from a lower rack and crouched in front of the safe, which had been bolted to the floor.

She tapped out the combination and the lock clicked while a green light flashed twice. She swung open the door of the safe and lifted out a .45 and a 9mm Glock. "Hold these."

Sam took the weapons from her, holding one in each hand, weighing them. He whistled through his teeth. "Nice."

Thumbing through two stacks of bills, she said, "It doesn't look like anything was taken from the safe."

"I suppose you don't have a camera inside or outside?"

"Nope." She sat back on her heels. "But maybe I need one."

"Not a bad idea." He held out the guns to her, handles first.

She placed the .45, a heavy piece, on top of the cash and slammed the door shut. She entered the combination again, and held her finger on the lock button until it beeped.

"You forgot the Glock."

"No, I didn't." She stood up to face him, clutching the gun in her hand. "I'm keeping this one with me."

"You do know how to use that thing, don't you?"

She slid open the chamber, checked the bullet nestled inside and closed it with a snap. "Sure."

"Do you think Wade found out you printed the map and broke in here to take it back? Did he have to break in? Does he know about the key under the flowerpot?"

"If he does, I never told him. His sister knows, but she wouldn't blab about that." She made a move to exit the closet and he stepped to the side.

Their little dance set her clothes into motion, the hangers clicking, the material whispering.

"And how would he know I printed out the map?" She exited the closet, the gun dangling at her side. "That's why I printed it instead of sending it to myself. *That* he would've noticed, but I don't think there's any trail when an image is printed from your phone, is there?"

"I don't have a clue." He pressed his thumb against the closet light switch. "Why wouldn't he want you to see the map? In fact, why did you go all cloak-and-dagger to get the map? You could've just asked him for a copy."

"I didn't want him to think I had any interest in the project beyond my initial rejection of it. That's why I was secretive about it. I don't know why he would be—unless there's something on that map he wants to keep hush-hush." She sank to the edge of her bed, thankful she'd had time to make it this morning.

He sat next to her, causing the mattress to dip and her shoulder to bump his. He didn't move. "Something illegal about the construction maybe? Did you notice anything about the map?"

She scooted away from him. "I don't know construction. I wouldn't have noticed anything like that. It was a building-phase map, which is why it helped me because it pinpointed exactly where the workers were going to start digging."

He patted his pocket. "I think your phone is ringing in the other room. It's not mine."

"It's probably Gran wondering what happened to me." She bounced up from the bed. "You can give me a ride?"

"Of course."

She snatched up her ringing phone on the counter, the call coming from Gran's friend Rosie. "Hello, Rosie?"

"Hi, Jolene. Viv is wondering when you're

going to pick up your car. I'm still here with her, so can you give me a ride back to town? Or I can drive the car to your place, and you can give me a ride home from there."

"I want to check in on Gran anyway, so I'll go out there. Sam can drive, and then take you home. He gave me a ride to my place. Is Gran okay?"

"A little wet, but just fine. We were wondering the same about you. Do they know where those bones came from?"

"That'll take a while, Rosie. Construction has been halted in the meantime."

"Okay, we'll wait for you and Sam."

Gran yelled in the background. "Tell her not to hurry."

Jolene rolled her eyes at Sam. "We'll see you in a little while, Rosie."

Sam scratched Chip's belly. "Granny Viv and Rosie took your car, leaving Rosie's grandson to take her car, leaving you to catch a ride home only to drive to the rez, get your car and give Rosie a ride home. Did I get that straight?"

"Maybe the scheme didn't work out quite the way Gran wanted it to, but at least we got to admit our secrets to each other and forge a plan."

"We forged a plan?" Sam stopped rubbing Chip, who kicked his legs in the air to show his displeasure.

"Of course we did, Sam Cross. We're going to

delay the Desert Sun Casino project long enough to find out if the land is the graveyard of missing people and why my father was murdered there."

As SAM PULLED his truck up in front of Gran's house, he tapped on the window. "Wade's here. That could be trouble."

Jolene narrowed her eyes as she stared at Wade's yellow Humvee. "Why does he drive that abomination?"

Sam shrugged. "I don't know. It must be good for maneuvering in the sand."

"Wrong answer." Jolene punched his rock-hard bicep. "Maybe I can hint around that I think someone broke into my house and watch his reaction."

"Not a great idea." Sam cut the engine on his truck. "Don't get into it with him at all. The man's gonna be on edge."

"The better to trap him." She yanked on the door handle and slid from the truck, avoiding a puddle of rain in the dirt.

As she and Sam walked up to the porch, her cousin stepped out of the house, all smiles.

"That was quite a ground-breaking ceremony this morning, wasn't it? Ended in dramatic fashion with a monsoon." Wade shook out his umbrella.

Jolene raised one eyebrow. "And a pile of bones."

"Well, it *is* the desert, right, Sam? There are bound to be bones buried in the desert." Wade skirted several pools of water with his expensive cowboy boots on his way to the Humvee. He grasped the handle and turned. "You know it's funny, though. We did survey that land thoroughly and didn't find any bones before, especially so close to the access road."

"Maybe your surveyors did a lousy job." She waved from the porch. "I'm sure you'll be back in the saddle in no time."

Wade touched his fingers to his forehead. "Count on it, cuz."

The Humvee's engine rumbled as Jolene grabbed the handle of the screen door.

Sam touched her ear with his lips. "He sure is cheery."

"It's a facade. He's running scared." She pulled open the screen door and knocked on the front door once before pushing her way in. "Gran, it's me."

Rosita rose from a chair, holding two coffee mugs. "We just had some tea. Do you want some?"

"I think Sam needs to get the truck back to the Border Patrol station, and I need to get my car." Jolene strolled to her grandmother's chair and dropped a kiss on top of her head. "Was I taking too long for you to wait for me, Gran?"

"I knew that storm was going to break any minute, and I figured you and Sam might want to catch up." She tilted her head back to look into Jolene's face. "I was right. You two took a while to get here."

Sam took the cups from Rosita's hands and carried them into Gran's small kitchen. "I stopped by Jolene's house to see Chip...the dog."

"How was Wade after that debacle at the ground-breaking ceremony?" Jolene perched on the arm of Gran's chair. "We just saw him outside, and he seemed to be taking it in stride."

"He was upset when he came over here to check on me, but he made a few calls and seemed to feel better after." Gran patted Jolene's knee. "He seemed to think you had something to do with the bones out there, Jolene. He came in here ranting and raving."

"Right. Like I have a spare skeleton in my closet at home." Jolene snorted. "Look, the Yaqui council voted, and they decided to go with the casino on that land. Nothing I can do about it."

"Your father could've stopped it." Gran clicked her tongue. "The rest don't have the backbone to stand up to Wade."

"Good thing Dad was conveniently murdered." Jolene blinked her eyes.

Gran's fingers turned into claws on Jolene's leg as she dug them into her flesh. "Wade loved your father, Jolene. He looked up to him. Learned from him. Please don't say those things to me."

"I'm sorry, Gran." Jolene kissed her grandmother's weathered cheek and stood up as Sam returned from washing the dishes in the sink. "Sam's going to give Rosie a ride back to her place, as they're heading in the same direction."

"Are you ready, Rosie?" Sam captured Gran's hand and kissed her gnarled fingers. "I'll see you later, Granny Viv."

"You can come by any time if you're washing dishes."

Rosie gathered her umbrella and purse and waved at Gran getting out of her chair. "Take a seat, Viv. We can see ourselves out."

Outside, Sam took Rosie's arm and steered her around the puddles to his truck as Jolene watched them, a hand on her hip.

After he handed Rosie into his truck, he approached Jolene. "What are you staring at?"

"You're such a gentleman…to the old gals."

"Hilarious." He placed his hands on her shoulders. "Be careful. Wade, or whoever, wanted that map back for some reason."

"Maybe he just wanted to make sure I didn't pull any stunts like the one today. I beat him to the punch, and now he's over it." She took a step back into Gran's house, hanging on to the screen door.

"Why wouldn't he just approach you? Tell you

he's aware you took the map from his phone, planted the bones and he's going to out you to the authorities?" He brushed some hair from her eyes. "There must be something else on that map he's hiding."

"Not sure I'll have another shot at it now." She waved to Rosie in the passenger seat of Sam's truck. "Thanks for the ride, Sam. Remember, I won't tell if you won't."

He pressed a finger to his lips and strode to his truck. She watched while Sam climbed in his truck and pulled out. As he peeled away from the house, he beeped his horn.

Jolene returned to Gran and spent the next hour giving her evasive answers about her and Sam. When she stood up and stretched, she gazed out the window at the rain coming down in sheets.

"I'd better get going, Gran. Do you need anything else?"

Gran patted her arm. "Just for you to be happy, Jolene."

She dropped a kiss on her grandmother's head. "Always that."

Outside, the rain lashed her as she ran to her car. She folded herself into the driver's seat and blasted the defroster. She rolled slowly along the roads of the reservation, and then turned onto the highway. The wipers on her car could barely keep up with the onslaught of water pouring across her windshield.

She sat forward in her seat, hunching over the steering wheel, easing off the accelerator. The car seemed to be floating underwater, the landscape a blurry, watery tapestry.

She picked up speed as she headed down an incline. She tapped her brakes and mumbled a few obscenities beneath her breath. The water had made her brakes squishy. She tapped again, putting a little more force into it.

As she stepped on the brake, the car whooshed forward, going even faster. She jerked the steering wheel harder than she wanted as she coasted into a slight curve in the road.

She tried the brakes again, and this time her foot hit the floor. Her back tires hydroplaned and the car began to fishtail. Gripping the steering wheel with one hand, she fumbled for the hand brake with the other.

The car lurched and skidded, and the rain-soaked scenery blurred into a kaleidoscope of colors as she careened out of control.

Chapter Six

Sam rolled to a stop in front of Rosie's neat Spanish-style house, the tiles on the roof dyed to a deep red from the torrent of rain, now moving sideways.

"Hold on a minute." He grabbed Rosie's umbrella and came around to the passenger side of the truck to let her out.

He held the umbrella over her head as he walked her to the front door.

Her grandson threw open the door. "Hurry, *Abuela*, before you get swept away."

Rosie turned to Sam on the porch. "You can take my umbrella back to the truck with you."

"That's okay." He handed the pink-and-red umbrella back to her. "I'm already wet. A little more rain isn't going to make much difference."

Head down, he jogged back to the truck. When he got behind the wheel, he flicked down the visor and slicked his hair back from his face, dripping with water.

He scowled at his reflection. "So much for drying your clothes at Jolene's."

It was a good ruse for taking half his clothes off at her place, anyway. Not that it did him much good. If he wanted to get back into her good graces…and her bed, he'd have to take things slowly. He'd burned her once, and she wasn't the type of woman who trusted easily—her mother's abandonment and her father's death had seen to that.

Then *he* had to pile on.

He shook his head like a dog, flinging drops of water inside the cab of the truck, and continued driving toward the station.

As he turned down the main street, he had to pull to the right for some emergency vehicles racing off to a call. A lot of people didn't know how to drive in a storm like this.

He started forward again and turned into the parking lot of the Border Patrol station, small compared to the one in San Diego, but Paradiso saw lots of action.

He nabbed a parking spot near the front door, as a skeletal crew was on Sunday duty, and half of them had been at the casino shindig. He ducked into the building and hung the keys to the duty truck on the appropriate peg.

One of the new agents popped his head up

from behind his computer monitor, his eyes wide. "Can you believe this storm?"

"It's monsoon season. Get used to it and enjoy the rain while it lasts."

Sam pulled up to his desk and brought up a map of the Yaqui land earmarked for the casino. He couldn't find anything online about the casino plans—at least nothing detailed. What could've been on that map that someone hadn't wanted Jolene to see?

He dug into his missing persons again, looking for any new links, but he just kept coming back to their involvement in the drug trade. They had to be dead, and their bodies had to be somewhere in the desert.

The phone jangled Sam's nerves even more, and Agent Herrera picked up. The agent's excited voice carried across the room.

When he hung up the phone, he scurried to Sam's desk. "Big accident on the highway. Car skidded off the road and went into the wash, which happens to be swollen right now."

Sam whipped his head around. "Did this just happen? I saw emergency vehicles on my way in."

"That was something else. This is a car in the wash."

A muscle ticked at the corner of Sam's mouth. "The highway north? Because I came from the rez, and I didn't see anything out that way."

"Yeah, north and this happened after you arrived."

"Do you know the make and model of the car?"

"Heard it on the radio—black truck."

Sam's heart thundered in his chest. "License plate?"

Herrera strode back to his desk and tapped his keyboard, a crease between his eyebrows. "No plates. The truck's partially submerged in water."

"Jolene Nighthawk drives a black truck, and when I left her, she was planning to head north on the highway." Sam snatched the keys from the peg where he'd left them just about an hour ago. "I'm taking the truck out to the accident. Let me know if you hear anything else."

"Will do."

Sam flew out of the station and got back in the truck. It took all his self-control not to speed off in the rain. He didn't need to get into an accident on the way to the site of one.

He swatted at a bead of sweat rolling down his face. Just because it was monsoon season in the desert didn't mean the temperatures dropped. The temps hovered in the high eighties despite the skies breaking open.

And he was feeling the heat.

As the storm moved through, the rain slacked off but his wipers were still working furiously to keep up with the water coursing across his windshield. He spotted the lights of the emergency vehicles before he could actually make out any shapes.

He eased off the accelerator and rolled to a stop behind a highway patrol car. Scrambling from his truck, he yanked out his ID and badge. As he passed the orange cones, an officer approached him and Sam flashed his badge.

"Any fatalities?"

The officer shook his head. "The woman escaped from her vehicle before it filled with water. It could've been a lot worse, but the wash isn't deep enough yet for a car to be completely submerged."

"Woman?" Sam got an adrenaline spike that made him dizzy. "She's okay?"

"She's a bit banged up, but she's fine." The officer pointed to two EMTs hovering at the back of their ambulance. "Over there."

Sam strode to the ambulance, glancing to his right at Jolene's black truck sitting upright in the water. As he approached, one of the EMTs stepped away to reveal Jolene sitting in the back of the ambulance, her feet dangling over the side.

Her eyes widened when she saw him. "Sam! What are you doing here?"

Warm relief washed through his body and he ate up the space between them in two long strides. He took her hands in his and brought them to his lips. "Are you all right? I heard about the accident involving a truck north of town and immediately thought of you. What happened?"

Her gaze darted toward the EMT unwrapping the blood pressure cuff from her arm. "I skidded off the road. I think my brakes locked up."

"Didn't I tell you to get a new car the last time I was here?" His nerves caused his voice to come out louder than he'd intended and with a sharp edge.

Jolene disentangled her hands from his. "You told me a lot of things the last time you were in Paradiso."

The EMT threw a sideways glance at Sam and said, "Ma'am, are you sure you don't want to go to the hospital?"

"I'm sure. The car slid off the road into the water, my airbag deployed and I was able to crawl out the passenger window. Just a few bumps with some bruises to follow, I'm sure." She held up her arms, displaying a red rash from the airbag. "You checked my vitals and I'm fine, right? I didn't hit my head, so no worries about a concussion."

A crane lifted her car from the wash and water poured out the windows and cascaded from the chassis.

The EMT pointed to the mess. "You're not driving off in that."

"I've got a Border Patrol agent right here with

his official truck to take me home." She patted his arm. "Right, Sam?"

"Absolutely, as long as she doesn't have any injuries and you don't think she's going to suffer any ill effects from the accident."

The EMT shrugged. "Just bruising, like she said. She has a few scrapes from squeezing through the window and clambering up the cement walls of the wash, but she acted fast—buzzed down that window and got out."

"Then we're good." Jolene hopped off the back of the ambulance and winced.

Sam caught her around the waist. "You sure you're okay?"

"Trent here already checked out my ankle. I just twisted it." She grimaced.

"Then you shouldn't be jumping around on it." Sam refused to release his hold on her, even though her body coiled away from his. "Do you need to talk to the cops?"

"They already got my statement—one car accident and no damage to public property."

"In that case..." He swept her up in his arms and carried her to his truck while she chattered in his ear.

"This is ridiculous, Sam. I don't need to be carried. Put me down, please."

He swung open the door of his truck and placed her inside. He hovered over her, hanging on the frame of the vehicle as the last of the storm spit out its final raindrops on the back of his neck.

"Let someone else take charge for a change." He leveled a finger at her. "You, sit."

He stomped off to find the cops investigating the scene of the accident and grabbed the first one. "Do you need Jolene anymore?"

The officer asked, "Is she leaving in the ambulance?"

"She doesn't want to go to the hospital. The EMTs cleared her, and I'm going to take her home. What happened out here?"

"Pretty much what she told us. She was driving in the rain, going downhill so her speed probably picked up. Her brakes failed, she applied her parking brake and the car spun out and landed upright in the wash. She was lucky. She called in the accident herself."

"That's good to hear. Her car being towed to the yard?"

"Yeah, they'll contact her, but it's probably totaled."

"Thanks." Sam pivoted away, took a few steps and called over his shoulder. "Brakes failed, huh?"

"That's what it sounds like."

Sam's boots crunched the soggy gravel as he returned to the truck. He climbed in and gripped the steering wheel with both hands. "Your brakes failed?"

"I stepped on the brake when I started going down the incline. Instead of slowing down, my car sort of whooshed forward. I didn't want to stomp on the brake pedal in the rain, so I eased my foot down and when it hit the floor, I knew I was in trouble."

A pain throbbed against his temple. "Were the brakes feeling squishy before? Squeaking?"

She tucked her hands beneath her thighs, and she hunched her shoulders as if warding off a shiver. "A little squishy, but I thought that was the rain."

"Your car's going to be towed to the police yard. It's totaled."

"The officers told me that. The tow truck driver gave me his info in case I need him for insurance purposes." She tapped a damp business card on the console. "What are you implying? About the brakes, I mean?"

He started the truck's engine and backed away from the patrol car before pulling onto the rain-slicked highway. "Brakes don't usually up and fail. You know it's coming. The pads go first, and you have that squishy, gummy feeling when you step on the brake. Brakes usually tell you they're failing by squeaking."

"So, if my brakes didn't gradually go bad on

their own, you're thinking someone made them go bad all at once?" Her knees started bouncing, and he placed a hand on one of them.

"Your car was sitting at Granny Viv's place while Wade was just there. Doesn't he know something about cars?"

"He has a few classic cars he tinkers with." She tilted her head. "I don't think my cousin would try to kill me. Besides, I saw him leave Gran's."

"He could've come back or had someone else do it. You didn't die. He couldn't know the brakes would go out in that spot by the wash, or that your car would spin out."

"If he wasn't trying to kill me, you think he was trying to warn me?"

That prospect didn't seem to bring her any comfort, as she laced her fingers together and twisted them.

"Maybe scare you off from interfering in casino business. He seems to know you were the one who planted the bones at the construction site. He knows you got your hands on that map and used it to throw a a into his opening ceremony." Sam shoved a wet lock of hair from his forehead. "Wade Nighthawk is a man on a mission—and I don't think he's going to allow you or anyone else to stand in his way."

"If he knows I left the bones there, he has to

know they're not going to come back as some ancient Yaqui."

"He also knows you, Jolene. He knows you're not going to give up. Maybe that accident was a little push to convince you to back off and leave it alone."

"Why doesn't he just tell me to my face?"

"Didn't he try that already?"

"Yes."

"He's never going to admit that he's behind any of this. He has a public persona to uphold, but make no mistake. If he had someone tamper with your brakes, he's fired a warning shot."

She gathered her hair in a ponytail and twisted it, squeezing out the water from the wash. "He should know better than that. I'm a Nighthawk."

As Jolene let Sam into her place, an ecstatic Chip circled their legs, his wet tail thumping out his welcome against the wall.

She patted his head. "He's been outside. I must've left the dog door open."

"Don't worry about Chip." He plucked at the sleeve of her blouse. "You're soaked to the bone. I don't care how warm it is. It's not a good idea to walk around in wet clothes."

"You should talk. I let you dry your clothes here and you got them all wet again." As she straightened up from petting Chip, a pain stabbed the back of her neck and she grabbed it, squeezing her eyes closed.

"Whiplash?" He cupped her elbow and led her to the couch. "That's why you go to the hospital when you're in an accident like that one."

"It's fine. I just feel a little banged up." She sank to the edge of the couch, her damp skirt clinging to her legs.

"You need a warm bath and a glass of wine." He backed up, tugging on Chip's collar. "Do you have any Epsom salt?"

"You're serious. You're going to run me a bath?" That's what worried her about Sam. He was all in—until he wasn't. He'd treated her like a princess, until he told her about his wife's pregnancy. A wife he'd supposedly separated from six months before, even though she was just three months pregnant.

"You don't climb out of an accident like yours and continue on as usual." He removed his gun from his holster and unbuckled his equipment belt.

"Oh, you mean business."

"I do. Stay there and relax."

She called after him. "No Epsom salts."

As Sam banged around in her bathroom, she twisted her head from side to side. Didn't feel like whiplash to her. She'd tried to relax her body when it became clear her car was going into the wash.

Could Wade really be responsible? She could see him issuing a warning, but he'd never try to seriously hurt her, would he? His ambition knew no bounds. He had his eye on politics, and he moved in the right circles.

"Look what I found." Sam returned to the living room with a pair of green Border Patrol sweats low on his hips, his upper body bare— again. When had he become such an exhibitionist?

She narrowed her eyes. "Where'd you find those?"

"Stuffed in your linen closet." He tugged at the waistband, pulling them even lower. "I remember giving you a few pairs of these."

"Yeah, I used to wear them." She got up too fast and clutched the back of the couch in her dizziness.

"You're not okay, Jolene. Are you sure you don't want me to take you to the emergency room?"

"No, thanks. You end up sicker from those places than you were when you walked in. I'm just a little rattled."

He joined her at the couch and slipped an arm around her waist. The brush of his bare skin against her arm overwhelmed her senses and her dizziness returned with a vengeance.

She leaned into him, and he tightened his hold on her.

"Let me help you."

He walked her into the master bathroom connected to her bedroom, past the pile of his wet clothes. A lilac-scented steam rose from the tub, foaming with bubbles.

"A bubble bath?"

"It's the closest thing I could find to Epsom salts. You can inhale the lilac like an aromatherapy thing." He'd flipped down the toilet seat and helped her sit.

When he reached around to unhook her skirt, she placed a hand on his arm. "I think I can get undressed by myself, Sam."

"Really? I'm not going to leave you and then hear a thud as you keel over, am I?" He unhooked and unzipped her skirt. "It's not like I haven't seen it all before."

She rested two fingers at the base of his throat where his pulse throbbed. "But you lost the privilege of seeing it all."

His dark eyebrows jumped, and his pulse beat faster against the pads of her fingers. "I did—and it was a privilege."

He stood up and started to back out of the bathroom. "Call me if you need help. I'll return with your wine."

He shut the door before she could tell him he

didn't have to bring the wine—not that she didn't need a glass or two about now. But she didn't want to tempt him if he were still on the wagon— and it looked as if he was.

She finished undressing and slipped into the silky water, releasing a long breath as the bubbles enveloped her.

When she'd met Sam two years ago, he'd just stopped drinking. She'd seen him at her cousin's AA meeting. She'd gone to a meeting with Melody to support her, and pretty much couldn't take her eyes off the blue-eyed, black-haired man who'd looked so indestructible as he talked about the problems alcohol had brought to his life.

Her own father had won his battle with the bottle and had been the strongest man she knew.

Melody had played matchmaker, and her first date with Sam had morphed from a coffee to dinner and three hours of conversation. She'd been wary at first. When hadn't she been wary with men? But Sam had won her over without even trying. Maybe it had been her desire to fix him. What grounded woman went into a relationship with a person battling addiction, even one in recovery, who'd just separated from his wife?

Sam tapped on the door. "Are you in the tub? No mishaps?"

"I managed to undress all by myself and climb in without toppling over."

He nudged the door open with his toe, carrying two glasses—a red wine for her and some iced tea for him. He sat on the edge of the tub, and she scooted farther under the bubbles.

He handed her the glass. "How does that feel? I didn't want to make it too hot."

"It's perfect, thank you." She wrapped her fingers around the stem of the glass. "You didn't need to bring me wine. Iced tea would've been okay."

"Don't worry about me." He took a sip of his tea and shook the ice in his glass. "Twenty-seven months sober. Not even a slipup."

"Congratulations. Melody, too." She tipped some wine into her mouth, letting it pool on her tongue before swallowing it. "Do you still go to meetings?"

"I hadn't been, but I'm not going to lie. I started attending more regularly at the time of the separation. It was hard leaving Jess, leaving her just like my old man left me, but your mother abandoned you, too, and you didn't turn to booze."

"Different situation, wasn't it?" She traced her finger around the rim of her glass. "I had my father and an extended family support system. Even though Dad turned to booze when Mom left, his illness gave me purpose. One of us had to be functioning."

Sam scooped up some bubbles, cupping them

in his palm before turning his hand over and watching them dislodge and float back into the tub. "Is that what you saw in me? Someone to fix like you'd fixed your dad?"

She caught her breath. Had he been reading her mind? She sliced her hand through the water like a shark's fin. "No. You'd already started your journey to recovery when we met."

"Ah, but it's a rocky journey filled with potholes and backtracking. Alcoholics are never really fixed, are we?"

"The minute I met you, I knew you'd be successful. I didn't think you'd need saving." The bubbles across her chest melted into the water, putting her closer to exposure. Did she care? What if she got in deep with Sam, and he left again? He had a daughter who had to take priority.

Could she have a fling with him while he was here? While they were in each other's confidence? Could she forget him once he left?

Sam dipped his hand in the water and swirled it dangerously close to her hip. "You're losing your bubbles, and this hasn't been very relaxing for you—digging up old stuff. Drink your wine with no guilt. Stop thinking about your dad, stop thinking about my problems."

"Stop thinking about my own?" She touched her glass to his and took a sip of wine, slipping farther beneath the lukewarm water. She reached out a hand and ran it down his bare chest to the waistband of the sweats. "There's plenty of room in here."

His Adam's apple bobbed as he swallowed. "You know I want that more than anything. I want you more than anything."

"But?"

"I want you to be sure. You hardly rolled out the red carpet when you saw me."

She lifted one eyebrow. "Consider the circumstances. I had just dumped some bones in a shallow grave."

"It was more than that." The tips of his fingers played along the peaks of the bubbles. "I hurt you. I lied to you. I broke your trust."

"I'm the one who told you to go away and be with your daughter."

"Because…"

Chip's barking interrupted him, and she was almost relieved. She didn't want to go down this road with him again. Either she could trust him or she couldn't…or it wouldn't matter either way.

She heaved a sigh. "Chip must've gone outside again. I hope he's not even more wet, or worse, muddy."

"I'll take care of Chip. Finish your wine and your bath." He pushed up from the side of the tub. "You should take some ibuprofen."

Chip's claws tapped across the tile floor, and he appeared at the bathroom door with something dangling from his mouth.

"What is that, Chip? Sam, what does he have?"

His tail upright and wagging, Chip advanced into the bathroom, his trophy clutched in his jaws.

Sam jumped back from the dog. "It's a snake."

Chip dropped the snake on the floor, and Jolene rose from the tub, her mouth hanging open. "It's not just a snake. It's a snake with an arrow through its head."

"What the hell?" Sam prodded the reptile with a bare toe. "At least it's dead. Who would kill a snake like that?"

Goose bumps raced across her bare flesh. "Someone sending a warning to another Yaqui."

Chapter Seven

Sam felt the hair on the back of his neck quiver. Someone out there was serious.

"Get it out of here, Sam."

He glanced at Jolene standing in the tub, water sluicing from her skin and bubbles clinging to strategic areas of her naked body.

Chip whined and pawed at the dead snake, so Sam gave him his due and patted his head. "Good dog. Good boy."

"Never mind Chip. Get that thing out of my bathroom."

"I got it." He stepped over the mess on the floor and took Jolene's slippery arm. "Sit back down. You're getting chilled."

"I think that's more from the snake than the air hitting my body." She glanced down, and a pink flush rushed from her chest to her cheeks, as if realizing for the first time she was standing naked in front of him.

She plopped back down in the water, creating waves that edged over the side of the tub.

"What does it mean? The dead snake?"

Crossing her arms on the edge of the tub, she hunched forward. "The legend of the snake people tells us that snakes can take the form of humans so to kill a snake, unless it's in self-defense, is evil. The arrow through the snake's head is a warning to all who see it that evil walks among us."

"So, someone delivering that dead snake to you is a message that you're dealing with some shady characters."

"Something like that. It's not a good sign any way you look at it." She slid back into the tub.

"I'm going to get a plastic bag and pick that thing up with a paper towel—just in case there are fingerprints. If this is a warning, then we need to know who's behind it."

"It's obvious, isn't it?" She scooped up water in her hands and dumped it on her chest. "Nobody but a Yaqui is going to understand the significance of a snake with an arrow through its head. It was Wade."

"Then it's time to confront him." Sam hooked two fingers in Chip's collar and pulled him out of the bathroom before the dog could destroy the evidence.

Sam pulled open a kitchen drawer and grabbed

a plastic bag. He ripped a sheet of paper towel from the roll and returned to the bathroom where Jolene was standing in a draining tub, a towel wrapped around her body.

He crouched next to the snake and picked it up by the arrow lodged in its head. He dropped the whole thing in the bag. "I'm gonna have prints run on that arrow, and then we'll have him."

"*If* he left prints." Jolene stepped out of the tub, avoiding the spot where Chip had dropped the snake. "This is ridiculous. If my cousin thinks he can get away with tampering with my brakes and leaving this warning, he's forgotten who I am."

"That's strange." Sam twisted the handle of the bag, tying it in a knot. "Why would Wade fix your brakes and then run over here and leave that message?"

"It's like you said." She tucked the corner of the towel under her arm. "He didn't expect my brakes to fail so spectacularly and maybe already planned to follow up with the snake warning as kind of a double whammy."

Sam scratched his chin. "You know what else is weird?"

"Besides you standing there making excuses for Wade?"

He jiggled the bag. "If nobody other than a Yaqui would understand the meaning behind the snake with the arrow, would Wade really do something so obvious?"

"You're asking these questions like my cousin is a normal person. He's unhinged. Why else would he act this way?" She pushed past him, the ends of her wet hair flinging drops of water at him.

"I don't think he's unhinged, Jolene. There's a lot of money at stake with this project. He's not about to watch it fail. That's why I don't think he'd do something as blatant as sending you that snake." He followed her into the bedroom. "I wonder where Chip found it."

Jolene turned in the middle of the room and flicked her fingers. "Out, please. I let you have a peek once, but don't get used to it."

He chuckled. "Yes, ma'am, but if you're running off to see Wade, I'm coming with you."

He exited her bedroom, dropped the bag with the snake on the counter so Chip couldn't get at it and returned to the bathroom to clean up. He rinsed out the tub and scooped up Jolene's wet clothes and dumped them in the hamper.

Turning, he nearly bumped into Jolene at the door. She'd changed into a pair of denim shorts and a red University of Arizona T-shirt. "Thanks for straightening up the bathroom. I heard the buzzer go off for the dryer. You can change out of your male stripper clothes and back into your uniform."

He spread his arms. "You think this is male stripper material? You need to get out more."

She tugged at the elastic waistband and let it snap back in place. "You don't need to wear these so low on your hips."

"I do if I want them to cover my ankles." He held up his foot. "No wonder I gave these to you."

He headed toward the laundry room and scooped his warm clothes from the dryer. He shook out his slacks and shirt and draped them over his arm.

"I'm going to get dressed in your room, if that's okay."

Jolene looked up from toweling off Chip. "Go ahead. Do you think Chip will lead me to the spot where he found the snake?"

"Maybe, but does it matter? You don't have a security system here, no cameras. Wade, or whoever, left it on your front porch or in your backyard or your driveway. He probably knew Chip would grab it."

She snorted. "Can you really picture Wade shooting a snake with a bow and arrow, and then creeping around my house with the thing in his hand? He had someone plant it. I'm sure of that, just like he had someone fix my brakes at the rez. There are plenty of young people who want to get in the good graces of Wade Nighthawk."

"We can always ask your neighbors if they saw someone lurking near your house."

"I'll ask around." She pointed to his uniform. "Get dressed. Then we'll pay a little visit to Wade."

Sam ducked into her bedroom and peeled off the sweats. He had a ways to go to win back Jolene's trust, but at least she'd put away those daggers that were in her eyes—a shared goal always helped.

When he came out of the bedroom tucking his shirt in his pants, Jolene greeted him, his equipment belt hanging from her fingertips.

"Hurry, this is heavy even without the gun."

"You *are* in a rush." He took the belt from her, looped it through his pants and reached for his weapon on the counter. "What's the hurry?"

"I want to catch Wade and Cerisse before they go out." She hitched her purse over her shoulder and slid the cover over the dog door. "I don't want Chip dragging in any more dead reptiles."

"You're really going to stride right up to his door and accuse him of killing snakes?" Sam opened the front door and poked his head outside. "Storm passed."

She pushed past him onto the porch. "One

storm passed but Wade has a whole other type of storm heading his way."

Twenty minutes later, Sam's truck navigated the curvy road up to the foothills. He tapped on the window. "If your brakes had failed on this road, you really would've been in trouble."

"Sliding into the wash wasn't enough trouble?" She crossed her arms. "I could've drowned."

"Don't remind me." He squeezed her thigh. "When I heard a black truck had been in an accident, my stomach dropped."

She threw him a sideways glance. "Really?"

"What do you think?" He snatched his hand back from her leg. "Did you imagine I stopped caring about you...ever?"

Massaging her right temple, she said, "I don't know what to think, Sam. I guess I never expected to see you back in Paradiso, and let's be honest. You didn't come here to see me. You're in Paradiso for your case, which happens to coincide with my interests."

He released a long breath. Too much, too soon. "Is Wade's house around the next bend?"

"The only one on that stretch—beyond the white gates. He's so pretentious." She huffed through her nose and dug her fingers into her biceps.

"Is this his money or Cerisse's? I know her

family is wealthy, but Wade did all right in the real estate business."

"A combination of the two. Her father got him started, and Wade took off."

"Is she Yaqui?"

"Half on her mother's side."

Sam slowed his truck and made a sharp right turn into a driveway bordered by towering saguaro cactus. He hunched over the steering wheel and whistled. "Nice place. I don't think I've ever been here before."

He pulled around the circular driveway behind Wade's Humvee and a shiny Tesla. Before he cut the engine, Jolene hopped out of his truck, the bag with the snake swinging at her side.

He scrambled after her, not sure what she had planned for her cousin. He stepped onto the porch behind her just as the last tones of the doorbell echoed on the other side of the double doors.

Cerisse opened the door, not a dyed-blond hair out of place, a serene smile curving her plumped-up lips. "Jolene, Sam, so nice to see you. Wade said you were back in town. To stay?"

"Border Patrol business. How are you, Cerisse?"

She parted her lips to answer, but Jolene pushed past her. "Where's Wade?"

Cerisse lifted one sculpted eyebrow. "Is he expecting you, Jolene?"

"Why? Do I need an appointment? He's my cousin. I knew him when he was sitting in the dirt, splashing in a rain puddle on the reservation."

"Jolene?" Wade trotted down the curved staircase, his long, thin fingers trailing along the polished bannister. "What's going on?"

"This." She ripped open the plastic bag Sam had carefully tied earlier to preserve the evidence, and dumped the dead snake on the floor. The point of the arrow clattered on the tile.

A scream pierced the air, and Sam jerked his head around as Melody flew down the stairs. "What is *that* doing in the house?"

"Ask your brother." Jolene clamped a hand on her hip. "He left it for me—after he tampered with my brakes."

Melody directed her wide-eyed gaze at Wade. "Wade? What is she talking about?"

"That's what I'd like to know." Wade spread his hands helplessly. "Sam?"

Cerisse touched Jolene's shoulder. "Do you want to sit down and explain, Jolene? You seem… overwrought."

"Oh, no you don't." Jolene shrugged away from Cerisse. "Somebody did something to my brakes today so that my car skidded in the rain, and I landed in the wash."

Melody gasped, covering her mouth with one

hand. "That was you? We heard about the accident."

"You think I fixed your brakes..." Wade smoothed a hand over his glossy ponytail "... and then doubled down by putting a warning on your porch?"

"I didn't say it was on my porch. Chip brought it in." Jolene tapped her toe, a staccato beat on the floor that only added to the tension in the room.

"Why would I do that, Jolene?" Wade hooked a thumb in the pocket of his black jeans.

"Y-you know." Jolene bit her bottom lip.

She hadn't thought this through enough to realize she'd have to admit to burying those bones at the construction site.

One corner of Wade's mouth lifted. "I don't. Please enlighten me."

"Those bones today." Jolene threw out a hand. "You think I had something to do with that. You think I'm trying to sabotage the casino project."

"Did you? Are you?" A slight twitch at the corner of his eye broke the smooth facade of Wade's face.

"Of course she didn't, Wade." Cerisse patted Jolene's back gingerly, as if Jolene were some kind of feral creature and one wrong move could set her off.

Sam didn't blame Cerisse one bit.

"I didn't plant those bones, but you know I'm

unhappy about the casino. My father wouldn't have wanted it, either."

"We've had this discussion before, Jolene. The casino will bring jobs. It'll improve the school on the reservation. All those things you *claim* to care about."

"My father died on that land. Don't you care about that?"

"I do, of course." Wade nudged the snake with the toe of his boot. "Could you please put this away? You're freaking Melody out."

"You can deny all you want, Wade, but I know you're behind these threats, these warnings." Jolene started to crouch down to shove the snake back in the bag, but Sam stopped her.

He bent over and pinched the snake's tail, dragging it back into the bag. The fewer fingerprints on this thing, the better.

"Cuz, if I thought you were interfering in the casino project, I'd just talk to you. In fact, I thought we already had that talk. You gave the impression that you were fine with it, or at least resigned to it."

"Just..." she shook a finger in his face "... watch yourself."

She spun around and charged outside.

Sam secured the bag again and shrugged. "She's upset about the accident. She had to squirm through the window into the water to get out of her car."

"That's terrible." Cerisse put a hand to her slender throat. "I'm glad you're back, Sam, if only for a short time. You always were the only one who could calm her down."

"She'll be fine." He raised his hand to Melody still clinging to the bannister of the staircase. "Good to see you again, Melody."

Always the gracious hostess, even in the most awkward of occasions, Cerisse showed him to the door with a smile. "Come back again under more pleasant circumstances."

Sam marched back to the truck where Jolene was already stationed in the passenger seat, her face tight. He'd better not tell her what Cerisse had said at the end there. She'd really explode.

He got behind the wheel, and placed the bag in the back seat. "That didn't go well. What did you expect? He wasn't going to admit it, even if he was responsible."

"If?" She pushed the hair from her flushed face. "You believed that smooth SOB?"

"Weren't you the one telling me after the accident that Wade wouldn't try to kill you?"

"Kill." She pounded a fist against her chest. "Do I look dead? He is trying to scare me off, though."

He cranked on the truck's engine and it rumbled in the circular driveway as he snapped in his seat belt. "Your feelings are out in the open now, so maybe that's not a bad thing."

"It's on you now, Sam. You have to find the bones of those missing people out there to put a stop to the construction."

"If I do find those remains, it'll halt the construction, but it's not going to stop it—not like it would if it were a sacred Yaqui burial site." He wheeled around the fancy cars in the driveway and rolled down to the street.

"I know that, but if the project goes on hiatus, I'll have some time to look around for clues to my father's murder. Once that casino goes up, any evidence is going to be lost forever." She sniffed and pulled one leg up to her chest, wrapping her arm around it.

"I know you think something's out there, Jolene, but the Pima County Sheriff's Department did a thorough investigation." He brushed a knuckle across her cheek.

"There has to be more. What was my father doing out there that night?"

"Maybe like you, he was searching for something that might put an end to the casino project." Sam lifted one shoulder.

"And maybe he found it."

He turned to face her, wondering if he should dissuade her from this line of thought or encourage it.

"Look out!" Jolene jerked forward and smacked her hand against the dashboard.

Sam slammed on the brakes before he twisted his head front and center. Melody waved from the side of the road.

"What the hell is she doing out here, and how'd she get here so fast from the house?" Sam eased off the brake, and the truck crawled toward Melody.

"She must've gone out the side of the house and bypassed the driveway, taking the shortcut to the road." Jolene buzzed down the window. "Are you crazy, Melody? We almost hit you."

Folding her arms, Melody tucked her hands against her sides and approached the truck. She ducked her head and peered at them through the open window, her dark hair with the pink streak creating a veil around her face. "I wanted to come out here and warn you to stop nosing around the casino project, Jolene."

"Great. You, too? I already got that warning, loud and clear, but it's not going to stop me. Something happened to Dad on that land, and I'm going to find out what it was before it's all covered over with slot machines."

"You don't understand, Jolene." Melody glanced over her shoulder. "Anyone who asks questions about the casino winds up dead—and you will, too."

Chapter Eight

As Sam pulled away from the side of the road in front of Wade's driveway, Jolene adjusted her side mirror to watch Melody grow smaller and smaller.

"What do you think about what she said? When we asked her, she couldn't name anyone else who had died as a result of snooping into the project. Do you think she's overreacting because of the snake? It really spooked her, but then Melody was always attuned to the old legends and myths."

"I hate to break it to you, Jolene, but Melody was drunk."

She tilted her head to the side to take in his profile. "Are you sure? She didn't seem drunk to me. Didn't smell drunk."

"Melody always favored vodka as her poison because it's hard to detect on someone's breath, but I saw the signs. You thought she was going to step in front of my truck because she was unsteady. Her eyes looked glassy, she slurred some of her words and…she was talking nonsense."

"You think so?" Jolene rubbed her hands against her bare thighs. "I wonder why she's drinking again. She told me she'd been clean and sober for years."

"Drunks can lie—and I should know. I'd be happy to go to a meeting with her while I'm here."

"What if she's telling the truth, Sam? Have there been any deaths associated with the casino project?"

"You're asking me? I haven't been in Paradiso for two years." He drummed his thumbs on the steering wheel. "But I can look into it. I haven't heard about any murders, except those associated with the drug trade."

"They wouldn't be classified as murders, would they? We can look for accidents, disappearances—I mean recent ones, not the ones you're looking at." She sat forward in her seat. "Where are we going?"

"When I heard about the accident on the highway, I took off in this Border Patrol truck. I still have my rental car at the station, and I want to drop off this bag—" he jerked his thumb over his shoulder "—to see if we can get any fingerprints from the arrow. Wade would have a hard time denying he put that on your property if we lifted his prints."

"What about me?" She trailed her fingers along

one arm that was showing signs of bruising from the airbag. "I don't even have a car."

"Will your insurance company give you a rental? Have you even reported the accident?"

"I was on the phone to my insurance agent one minute after I called 911 and two minutes after I crawled from the wash like some swamp creature, before you came on the scene. They'll pay for a rental."

"This has been a helluva day, starting with the casino opening ceremony. Have you eaten anything since those few spoonfuls of chili you scarfed down at the ground-breaking?"

"No, but our day isn't over yet." She dug her phone out of her purse, which was still wet from the accident. "We're going to check out those deaths."

He pointed to her phone. "Does that still work?"

"It was zipped inside my purse when I brought it to the surface with me. I used it to call 911." She flashed it at him. "And now I have a text coming in from my insurance company."

"You could do a commercial for that phone. And when I mentioned looking into the deaths, I didn't mean right this minute."

"No time like the present."

He grunted, which she took as agreement.

She glanced at him as he made the turn onto

the main street running through town. Was he agreeing to all this because he believed her, believed Melody or was he doing it to stay close to her? Did it matter?

"All of this can only help your own case. You can't go digging around private Yaqui property, a construction site, because you have a hunch. If we discover additional…irregularities with the casino project, we can delay it even further."

"Okay, we're here." He pulled up to the Border Patrol station and parked the truck with the other official vehicles.

She had her own government truck with the National Park Service, but she didn't use it for personal transportation, either. Rubbing the side of her head, she said, "I have work tomorrow."

"Don't be ridiculous. You were in a bad car accident today. Call in sick for a few days." He tapped his head. "Does that hurt?"

"I do have a headache."

"So much for relaxing in a warm tub with a glass of wine." He cocked his head. "You sure you don't want to see a doctor?"

She pulled at the door handle and said, "I want to get to the bottom of what's going on at the property."

Once inside, Sam darted around the mostly empty office, preparing the snake and arrow for a fingerprint request and packing up his laptop.

After Jolene called her boss at the Park Service, she wandered among the desks. She picked up a framed photo of Nash Dillon, his fiancée and their baby.

"Have you seen Nash's baby yet? He and his fiancée are adopting."

"I heard that and couldn't believe it. I sort of thought he was a confirmed bachelor."

"The baby's mother was murdered—involved with a drug dealer. Jaycee Lemoin, she was from Paradiso, but not while you lived here." She put the picture down and sighed. "So much misery."

"I know about that situation." He shoved his laptop into his case. "I'm ready to get out of here, but I need to eat and change, not necessarily in that order. If we go out, I need to change first."

"Can we pick something up or order in? I'm really anxious to see if there have been any other unexplained deaths lately."

"Any others?"

"Besides my father." She leveled a finger at him. "And don't start with me. I never believed he was killed by drug dealers. Why? He was on Yaqui land. Why would the cartels be out there?"

"Good question." He placed a hand over his chest, over his heart. "And I wasn't going to say a word. There's definitely something going on with that project."

"Y-you haven't heard anything about the bones yet, have you?"

"Nothing." He slung his computer case over one shoulder. "You didn't leave anything that can be tied to you, did you?"

"No." She put a finger to her lips and rolled her eyes toward the other agent on the phone.

Sam called out to him and raised his hand. "Out of here, Herrera."

The agent waved them off and kicked his feet up on his desk.

As Sam opened the door for her, he said, "I don't think he was listening to one word we said, not that he could hear us."

"It's better to be careful. I don't want to be arrested for…illegally dumping bones."

He squeezed the back of her neck. "Nobody is going to arrest you."

"Desperate circumstances call for desperate measures, and that's all I could think of doing to halt that construction short of sabotaging the equipment."

"That—" Sam beeped the remote for his rental car "—*would* get you arrested. Promise me you won't do something like that."

"I promise. I'm not sure I would even know how to go about doing that."

"I'm sure you'd think of something." He opened the passenger door for her. "Pick up or delivery?"

"I'm okay with a pizza delivery. You?"

"I'm so hungry I could've eaten that dead snake." He slammed her door and opened the other side seconds later.

As he pulled out of the parking lot, he asked, "Is it just because your father died there that you want to stop this construction? From everything I hear, it's going to provide jobs. If there were any endangered species on that land or the construction was going to be a threat to any species, you'd know that by now, right?"

"That's right. The studies have been done. I even participated in them. Nothing's going to suffer out there. My father was opposed to it because he wanted the desert to remain in its natural form, but even he recognized the importance of the jobs. I think he would've come around eventually. That's why I can't understand what happened. Wade and his cronies would've had a more difficult approval process had my father been alive, but I think even Wade knew my father would have given in eventually once all the studies came back."

"You think he might've been killed for some other reason?"

She lifted her shoulders to her ears. She couldn't explain her conviction to Sam. She had no facts, just feelings. "Maybe."

"Drugs."

"We're back to that?" She pulled her phone from her purse and cupped it between her hands.

"Because it makes sense, Jolene. He could've witnessed something, found something. There's a reason the sheriff's department came to that conclusion." He tapped her hand. "Are you going to order that pizza?"

"Do you want anything else? Salad?"

"Basic pepperoni is fine or whatever else you want on it. I don't need salad."

Sam pulled into the parking lot of his motel and cut the engine. "Do you want to come in? I'll be just a minute."

"I'll wait in the car and order the pizza."

As he hustled to his room, she phoned in their order for a large pepperoni pizza. Two minutes after she ended the call, Sam appeared in the parking lot, his green uniform swapped out for a pair of light-washed jeans and a dark blue T-shirt she just knew matched his eyes.

He settled behind the wheel and asked, "Pizza ordered?"

"One-track mind. Yes, I ordered the pizza. Let's get back to my place so we can start our search."

"One-track mind."

As they drove past the scene of her accident, Sam rapped a knuckle on the window. "This is where your car went off the road. I can just make out the skid marks. That was a close call. What do you think of Wade's response when you accused him of fixing your brakes?"

"Deny, deny, deny." She kicked off her sandal and wedged a bare foot on his dashboard. "I didn't expect anything else, but I put him on notice. When are you going to return to the construction site? You'd better make a move before the powers that be discover the bones today don't mean much of anything."

"I'll make my way out there. Don't worry about it." He rolled up to her house and swung into the driveway. "Are you going to get yourself a rental car tomorrow?"

She patted the side of her purse where she'd stashed her phone. "I've already made arrangements through text."

He parked the car, and she jumped out to search the porch before unlocking the front door. "No more presents."

She eased open the door, and Chip stuck his nose in the crack. "Yes, I brought Sam back with me. Don't worry."

As Sam stepped through the door, Chip pranced around his legs, wagging his chocolate brown tail a mile a minute.

How easy it was to be a dog. Chip could show his unbridled enthusiasm for having Sam back without risking heartache. It just wasn't feasible to have unconditional love for someone, not if you wanted to protect yourself.

And she wanted to protect herself against Sam.

Sam hauled his laptop onto her kitchen table. "We'll work here until the pizza comes."

"I'm going to feed Chip while you're setting up. Are we going to be able to see all deaths in the Paradiso area for the past two years? I think that's what we need to look at."

"We can do that." He flipped up the cover on his laptop. "We can also search for Desert Sun Casino opposition."

"Good idea." She ducked into the laundry room where she kept Chip's dog food in a plastic bin. She scooped out two cups for him and brought his dish into the kitchen where she added some warm water to the kibble.

She nudged his furry body with her knee. "You think you should be rewarded for bringing in that snake, huh?"

Sam looked up from his computer. "He can have some pepperoni from the pizza."

"That's not good for him. No wonder he lost a little weight after you…left." Her voice hitched, and she balled up a fist and pressed it against her stomach. Chip hadn't been the only one who'd lost weight.

Sam made kissing noises in the air. "Aww,

what's the matter boy? Your mom doesn't spoil you?"

Chip turned his back on his food and trotted over to Sam.

"Do you mind? I'm trying to feed him." She gave a sharp whistle and shook Chip's bowl before setting it down on the kitchen floor.

Chip twirled around and made a beeline for his dish.

Jolene eyed the bottle of red Sam had opened earlier, and then pulled open the fridge. "Do you want something to drink with your pizza? Iced tea, lemonade, soda, water?"

"Water's fine—and stop making goo-goo eyes at that wine and pour yourself a glass. Do you think the smell of alcohol is going to make me relapse?"

"It's not rude?"

"Was it rude before when we were...dating? You drank then, and I didn't have a problem with it. I'm further along in my sobriety now, and it's even less of a problem."

She uncorked the bottle and plucked the wineglass she'd used earlier from the dish drainer. She poured half a glass, glanced at Sam hunched over his laptop and splashed in a few more gulps.

As she filled up a glass of water for Sam, the doorbell rang, setting Chip into a frenzy.

Sam hopped up from the table. "Settle down, Chip. We don't wanna scare away the pizza guy."

He got the door and paid the bill. As he carried the box to the kitchen, Chip went back to his own food.

Sam dangled a plastic bag from his fingers. "Paper plates and napkins?"

"I asked for those, too. We don't need to worry about dishes on top of everything else." She flipped open the box and loosened two slices from the whole. She plopped them onto a plate and put another two onto the other plate.

"You can add a few more of those for me." Sam rubbed his hands together. "Pizza from Mr. Pizza—one of the many things I missed about Paradiso."

"There's no pizza in San Diego?" She loaded Sam's plate with another two slices and carried the food to the table while Sam grabbed the drinks.

He said, "There are some things in Paradiso that you just can't get in San Diego."

She jerked her head around and raised her eyebrows. "You're pretty slick, Sam Cross."

"Don't get too full of yourself, Jolene Nighthawk." He raised the glasses. "I meant the pizza and… Chip."

She placed his plate next to the computer and took a seat.

"If you think I'm going to ruin my dinner by working, you don't know how hungry I am." He shoved the laptop to the center of the table and stationed himself in front of his food.

He wolfed down one piece before coming up for air and taking a drink of water.

Jolene swirled her wine. "I don't think I've ever seen anyone inhale a slice of pizza that fast in my life."

"Did I mention I was starving?" He plucked a circle of pepperoni from a slice on his plate and fed it to Chip, waiting patiently by Sam's chair.

"Hey! Chip doesn't need pepperoni."

"Look how happy he is." Sam patted Chip's head, and then wiped his hands on a paper napkin. "Now that the edge is off, I can take a look at this database—over another piece of pizza."

Still seated, she scooted her chair around next to his. "Are these the deaths for the past few years?"

"Sorted by most recent, first." He poked his finger at the screen. "Name, address, manner of death—so, homicide, suicide, accident, natural causes and some other stuff that I can collapse."

She tore the corner off her pizza with her teeth and loomed over Sam's shoulder, scanning the lines that contained too much information. "This is confusing."

"You're getting crumbs on my laptop." He blew

on the keyboard. "And you're chewing in my ear. Give me a few seconds to get rid of some of these columns we don't need to see. When we pare this down, we can click on the file number and it'll take us to another database with more information about the details of the death."

Drawing back, she reached for her wine and took a sip. "You're not going to get into trouble for logging in and using these programs, are you?"

"I'm in Paradiso to investigate links between some missing people here and the remains of the missing people we located in the desert east of San Diego. Why wouldn't I be accessing these databases?" He clicked around the page, cleaning up the table, distilling it to the pertinent information.

She waved her hand at the screen. "Do you think we should eliminate the people over a certain age who died of natural causes?"

"We can do that." He scrolled down the list. "Here's an eighty-six-year-old woman who had a stroke."

"Yeah, like those." She squinted at the cause of death column. "More homicides than you'd expect outside of Tucson and Phoenix."

"Courtesy of the border and the drug trade."

They worked on the database together for over

an hour and managed to polish off the pizza at the same time.

Jolene had limited her wine consumption to one glass, even though she could've used another. She collected the paper plates and the glasses.

"I think we have a good list to start going through. We already know we can ignore the murders of Jaycee Lemoin, her boyfriend, Brett, and the social worker he killed. Those didn't have anything to do with the casino project."

"Maybe none of these did." Sam lifted his head. "Is that your phone or mine?"

"Oops, mine." Jolene tossed the plates into the empty pizza box and grabbed the phone, flashing an unknown number. "Hello?"

"Jolene?"

"Yeah, who's this?"

"This is Eddie, the bartender at the Sundowner."

She raised her eyebrows at Sam. "Yeah, I know you. What's up, Eddie?"

"Your cousin Melody is at the bar and she's lit. I tried calling Wade, but he's not picking up."

"What's she doing?" She mouthed Melody's name to Sam. "Can you call her a rideshare?"

"Normally I'd do that but she's in bad shape, Jolene. I'm afraid to let her out the door by herself, and I don't trust any of these guys here tonight. They're not much better off themselves.

I'd take care of her myself, but I have another two hours of work and she can't stay here in her condition."

"Okay, I'll be right over. Thanks, Eddie." She ended the call and tapped the phone against her chin. "You were right. Melody's fallen off the wagon—and in spectacular fashion. Sounds like she's drunk and disorderly in the Sundowner."

"Great." Sam logged off the computer. "I'm coming with you. Maybe I can talk her down."

"Let Chip out for a few minutes while I clean up the kitchen." She shoved the napkins in the pizza box. As she walked past Sam, she handed him the box. "Can you throw this in the trash outside, please?"

When Chip came back inside, Jolene locked up the house and grabbed her purse. As they walked out to Sam's rental car, she said, "I'm so disappointed in her."

Sam opened her car door and placed a hand on her shoulder. "You're not more disappointed than Melody is. Remember that. She already feels like a failure. Don't make it worse for her."

"You're right." She twisted her head to the side, and kissed the hand that rested on her shoulder. "I'm glad you're here."

Sam's eyes flickered for a second.

She'd meant it, at least for now.

The Sundowner had been a staple of Paradiso

nightlife when Sam lived here two years ago, not that it was ever a place he frequented. He'd already stopped drinking and had separated from his wife by the time he moved here.

When she'd met him, he'd fallen off the wagon once, three months into his six months of sobriety—and that misstep had resulted in his ex's pregnancy. He'd told her about going back on the booze, but had failed to mention the hookup with his ex.

Not that she'd known him at the time. They'd gotten together a few months after that, and had had a few more blissful months until he announced that his ex was pregnant, which had signaled the end of their love story.

Sam nudged her shoulder. "It's at the end of the block, right?"

"The place with the blue-and-red neon sign."

"It's busy." Sam cruised past the front and all the cars parked along the curb and a rideshare double-parked, waiting for its rider.

"I'll make a U-turn." He turned the car around at the end of the block and parked across the street.

They got out of the car, and Sam grabbed her hand as they ran to the other side of the street.

Smokers had spilled out of the bar onto the sidewalk where live music from a country rock band blared. They squeezed past a drunk stumbling out the front door.

"I hope she's not in the same condition as that guy." Jolene jerked her thumb over her shoulder.

"If she is, we can handle it." Sam peered over everyone's heads.

She tugged on his sleeve, as the bass from the band reverberated in her chest. "See her?"

"No, let's head to the bar and find Eddie. Do you know what he looks like?"

"Big guy, shaved head, long beard and pumped-up, tattooed arms—can't miss him."

"Got him. He's a busy guy. Nice of him to take the time to call you." Sam steered her through the crowd, and they edged up to the bar.

Jolene raised her hand. "Eddie!"

The big guy nodded once as he topped off a beer. When he finished with his customer, he moved down the bar and stopped on the other side from them, folding his massive arms. "She's gone."

"Gone? Where?" Jolene scanned the heads around her, hoping to see her cousin's pink-streaked black hair.

"She ordered a rideshare on her phone. I told her you were coming, but she didn't want to see you." He swiped the counter with a white cloth. "You know, she's been hitting the bottle for a while, but didn't want you to know."

"I'm not here to judge her. I just wanted to make sure she's safe." Jolene hugged her purse to her chest. She was pretty sure she'd vented to Melody about drunks who relapsed when she found out about Sam and his ex—maybe once or twice.

"She was coherent enough to order the car?" Sam braced his hands against the bar.

Eddie answered, "I helped her when she made it clear she was going home by herself, even though I tried to talk her out of it. You just missed her."

"Thanks, Eddie. I appreciate it." Jolene slipped her phone from the side pocket of her purse and called Melody's number. She listened to three rings before Melody's voice mail answered.

"She's not answering—probably because she saw it was me."

Sam cocked his head. "How many people use rideshare around here?"

"From the bar?" Eddie tugged on his earlobe, elongated with multiple piercings. "A good number. Hey, I gotta get back to work. Hope Melody is okay. I got a soft spot for that crazy girl."

Sam turned and leaned his back against the bar. "Does Melody live with Wade?"

"No, she has her own place. We should stop by, huh?"

"For sure. When Eddie called you, he didn't

seem convinced Melody could make it home on her own safely. I think it's a good idea to check in on her."

"I agree." She tipped her head toward the band on the stage. "They're not bad."

Sam cut a bigger swath through the crowd than she could, so he led the way while she hooked a finger in the back pocket of his jeans.

As they burst onto the sidewalk, Sam dragged in a deep breath. "That smell makes me sick now."

She stepped off the curb, and he grabbed her arm.

"Hold on. That rideshare car is still waiting." He strode down the sidewalk and ducked down to the open passenger window of the car. "Who are you picking up?"

The driver pointed at Jolene standing next to Sam. "Are you Melody?"

Jolene put a hand to her throat. "You're waiting for Melody?"

"Is that you?"

"She's my cousin. I came to pick her up, but the bartender said she'd ordered a car. You're telling me she never came out here?"

"I don't know if she ever came out here or not, but nobody named Melody ever claimed the ride." He tapped the phone mounted on his dashboard. "I gave her fifteen minutes, so I'm gonna bounce and pick up another ride—unless you need a lift."

"N-no."

She and Sam backed away from the car and stared at each other.

"What does it mean?" She licked her lips. "She ordered a car and didn't take the ride?"

"Maybe someone she knew saw her and took her home." Sam placed his hand on the small of her back. "Now we really need to go to her place."

She swept her arm to encompass the people scattered on the sidewalk. "Should we ask them if they saw her?"

"We can try."

With Sam at her elbow, she questioned the people on the sidewalk, but nobody remembered seeing a woman with pink-streaked hair, although one of the smokers remembered her from inside the bar.

He flicked his cigarette butt into the gutter and grinned. "That chick was wasted—tequila. Had to be tequila."

"But you didn't see where she went when she left the bar?"

"Sorry, no. She left before I did."

Jolene's heart hammered in her chest as she crossed the street with Sam. "I hope she's home safe, but why isn't she answering her phone?"

"You tried again?"

"I can't." As she settled in the car, she pulled

out her phone and shook it from side to side "It's dead. Maybe it did get damaged in the accident."

"Use mine. I think I still have her number in my phone if you don't have it memorized." He handed his phone to her and then went around to the driver's side.

Jolene found Melody's number in Sam's phone and tapped it. This time it went straight to voice mail with no ring.

When Sam got behind the wheel, she grabbed his arm. "Sam, I think her phone is off now. It went straight to voice mail without ringing. Why would her phone be off?"

"Maybe it died when she got home. Maybe she turned it off."

"That girl never turns off her phone. It's attached to her hand."

"She's drunk, Jolene. It could mean anything." He started the car. "Which direction is her place?"

She guided him to Melody's apartment in one of the new buildings that had gone up to house workers coming in for the pecan-processing plant.

"She's on the second floor." She pointed through the windshield as Sam parked the car near the edge of the parking lot, away from tenant parking. "That's her place up there. She has a light on."

"She's probably passed out on the floor, or maybe she got lucky and made it to her bed.

Worst-case scenario, she's clutching the toilet seat, puking her guts out."

"I'll take that worst-case scenario."

Sam's mouth tightened as he walked up the stairs to Melody's. Did he really believe his own worst-case scenario?

When they reached the second-floor landing, Jolene gasped. "That's her door, the one that's open."

Sam put his arm out. "Stay back for a minute and let me check it out."

With her adrenaline coursing through her system, Jolene pushed past Sam and charged through Melody's front door.

"Melody?" Jolene tripped to a stop and smacked her hand against a wall to steady herself. "Sam, she's been hurt. She passed out. There's blood."

Sam eased past Jolene and crouched next to Melody. He put two fingers against her throat.

"How bad is it? We need to call 911." Jolene took a step toward Sam.

"Stop. Don't come any closer. Melody is dead."

Chapter Nine

Jolene's face turned white, and her hand slid down the wall as she collapsed to a crouch. "Are you sure?"

"She doesn't have a pulse. CPR isn't going to help at this point." Sam put a finger on Melody's chin, her flesh still warm, and tipped her head to the side. Blood from a deep gash matted Melody's hair. "It's a head injury."

Jolene plunged her hand into her purse. "I'm calling 911."

"Your phone's dead." He held out his phone to her. "Try not to touch anything in here, Jolene."

As Jolene spoke a rush of words to the 911 operator, Sam swiveled his head to take a look around the room. As far as he could tell, nothing had been disturbed. Then he noticed blood on the edge of a glass coffee table. Squinting, he leaned in, careful not to touch it.

Jolene ended the call. "They're on their way. What happened, Sam?"

"There's blood and a few strands of hair stuck to that table. It's the right shape. She could've fallen and hit her head on the table."

"That would be enough to kill her?" Jolene sawed at her bottom lip with her teeth, her eyes wide and glassy.

"Do you see Melody's phone? Her purse?" Sam inched away from the body. He had to get Jolene out of here. If there was any foul play, they didn't want to be tromping around a crime scene.

Still gripping his phone, Jolene asked, "Do you think this was some kind of robbery gone wrong? Melody walked in on someone, and he pushed her? Took her purse?"

"I don't know. Do you see the purse?"

"Melody always carried a small cross-body bag, It's not…on her?"

Sam glanced down at Melody's still form, her pink-streaked hair fanning across her face. His gaze tracked across her blouse, bunched around her waist, her skirt demurely smoothed over her thighs and her feet with one sandal on and one off. "I don't see a purse."

Jolene twisted her hair into a knot over her shoulder. "How could this happen? We just missed her at the bar."

"Things happen when you're drunk. Things happen when you're drunk…and know too much." Sam pushed up to his feet. "I hear the sirens. We need to step outside."

Jolene seemed frozen in place. "Do you think someone killed her? That was my first thought, but I didn't want to come off as paranoid."

"Then we're both paranoid." Sam held out his hand. "C'mon. You already got your prints on that wall."

"I'm a visitor here. My prints are going to be all over this apartment." She grasped his hand with her cold fingers and he drew her up as the sirens ended in the parking lot below.

"We'll let the police figure it out."

"Like they figured out my father's murder?" She shook her head. "They'll take the path of least resistance. Her purse is missing, and she was drunk. That will be their main focus."

"Whoever took her purse and phone must've turned it off. That's why you couldn't get through the last time you tried from my phone."

Footsteps clumped up the stairs, and Sam led Jolene out of the apartment just as the first responders made it to the landing.

Sam raised his hand. "Over here."

The next thirty minutes were a blur of activity. The EMTs didn't try to revive Melody, as they'd discovered the same thing he had—no pulse.

How had that happened so fast? Melody had lost a lot of blood, but not enough to bleed out in twenty minutes. The blow to her head could've done her in immediately. Had someone hit her and then smeared her blood and hair on the table to make it look like an accident?

How many other deaths in that database were conveniently accidental?

Jolene had wandered back into the apartment when the EMTs called it quits on Melody. The crime scene investigators from the sheriff's department were too busy to notice her presence. He hoped she wasn't in there contaminating evidence. Maybe she just didn't want to leave Melody alone.

The officer Sam had been talking to came up the stairs again. "The medical examiner is on her way. I don't have anything else for you or Ms. Nighthawk. You have my card, and I have your phone numbers. We'll be in touch if we need anything else."

Sam pointed to the eaves running above the apartment doorways. "Too bad there are no cameras here."

"We might be able to get something from across the street, and even though we don't have her phone, we'll get those records and see if she ordered another car."

"I'll be in Paradiso for a while on my case, so keep me apprised. Jolene, Ms. Nighthawk, is understandably devastated by the death of her cousin."

"She's Wade Nighthawk's sister, too." The deputy pointed down to the parking lot where Wade was talking to a uniformed cop. "Wade has friends in high places. Someone must've told him."

Sam hustled back to Melody's apartment and called to Jolene, who seemed transfixed by the CSI guys going through Melody's living room.

She jerked her head to the side. "I—I just don't want her to be alone."

"I know." He crooked his finger at her. "Come here a second."

She gave a last look at Melody and approached him, tears streaking her face. She must've come out of the shock that had gripped her when they first discovered Melody.

He wrapped his arms around her and whispered in her ear. "Wade's here."

Her body stiffened, and he patted her back. "Don't make any wild accusations against him— not here, not now. That's his sister lying there."

She nodded and buried her face in his shoulder. "We should've done more."

"I know."

As Sam drew her out onto the landing, Wade shouted. "What are you two doing here? They won't let me pass."

Sam steered Jolene toward her cousin. "We found her, Wade. The bartender at the Sundowner called Jolene to pick up Melody, and we got there too late."

"How'd she get home? Who did this?" Wade's smooth face had tightened into a mask. His dark eyes glittered with anger.

Jolene hugged her cousin. "We don't know, Wade. We think she took a rideshare home. H-her purse is missing."

"I told her not to live here on her own." Wade smacked a fist into his palm. "She could've lived with us."

With her arms still wrapped around Wade, Jolene asked, "When did she start drinking again?"

Sam held his breath.

"Don't blame me for that. If you weren't so busy running around with your head in the clouds, you would've noticed. I couldn't make her stop." He thrust his hand out toward Sam. "Ask your boyfriend there if anyone can get an alcoholic to stop drinking."

Sam clenched his jaw, and then rolled his shoulders. The man had just lost his sister. "He's right, Jolene. Nobody is to blame for Melody's drinking except Melody."

"You're both accusing me of something I didn't even say." Jolene folded her arms. "I'm not blaming you. If anyone's to blame, it's me. If we had gotten to the Sundowner faster, we could've given Melody a ride home. Sam would've seen her safely inside."

"Look, I'm sorry. Sorry, Sam." Wade wiped

his brow with the back of his hand. "I'm upset, lashing out."

Wade smoothed his hand along his ponytail, and his chest heaved as he took a deep breath. The smooth politician emerged. "Do the police think it was a robbery or an accident? All they told me was that she died from a head injury. Did she fall, or did someone hit her? They didn't tell me her purse was missing."

The medical examiner's white van pulled into the parking lot, and Sam touched Wade's arm. "Let's go downstairs, and let them finish their work here."

Wade gestured to the neighbors poking their heads out their doors. "Did anyone hear anything? See anything?"

Jolene answered, "We don't know, but the officers questioned them. They wouldn't tell us anything. The apartment next to Melody's is vacant. I remember when her neighbor moved out of there a few months ago. The management company hasn't rented it out yet."

They reached the bottom of the stairs and stepped aside for two people from the medical examiner's van carrying a stretcher.

Jolene averted her face as Wade swallowed, a struggle to maintain control twisting his features for a minute.

"The officers said they might be able to get

something from the cameras over there." Sam pointed across the street.

"This damned building didn't even have a security system or cameras." Wade squeezed his eyes closed. "I told her. I told her."

Jolene took her cousin's hand. "Was Melody seeing anyone? Would someone else have picked her up from the bar?"

Wade's lids flew open. "What are you saying? Don't the police think this is either an accident or a robbery? You're not suggesting someone murdered Melody, are you?"

"I don't know." Jolene shrugged. "I'm just asking a question, and it's still murder if it was committed during a robbery."

"You would probably know more about Melody's dating life than I would. She didn't tell me anything like that, not after…"

"Not after you chased off the last guy." Jolene held up her hands. "I'm just saying."

"He was bad news, and you know it, Jolene. He's probably the one who got her drinking again."

"Is that true, Jolene?" Sam's hands curled into fists. "If so, Wade's right—bad news."

"I don't know. I don't think so. Melody and that guy split up almost six months ago. I don't think she'd been drinking that long." Jolene ran a hand through her hair. "Or maybe I'm just clueless."

"I don't know." Wade stared over Sam's shoulder, his eyes blinking. "I have to go up and see Melody's…body. I want to see her."

"Of course you do." Jolene squeezed his hand. "Let me know if we can do anything."

They both watched Wade's stiff back as he walked to the apartment's staircase, still swarming with cops.

Melody rubbed the back of her hand across her nose. "He seemed upset—or Wade-upset, which is a little different from everyone else's upset."

"I don't think Wade would murder his own sister—pay her off, threaten her, coerce her—but not murder." Sam pinched the bridge of his nose. "I have a headache, and I can't even imagine what you're feeling. I'm sorry about Melody, Jolene. Like the bartender said, I always had a soft spot for Melody, too. She's the one who introduced me to you."

He hit the remote for his car, and Jolene glanced at him from beneath her lashes before following him to the passenger side.

As he opened her door, a hissing sound came from the bushes bordering the parking lot. Sam pivoted and peered into the foliage, as Jolene tucked her fingers in the waistband of his jeans.

As he stepped in front of Jolene, Sam barked, "Who's there?"

A pair of eyes gleamed from a face that appeared between two bushes. "Hey, you ain't the po-po, are you?"

Sam knew how to answer that question under these circumstances. "No, I'm not a cop. Why? Who are you?"

The man shuffled from his hiding place, twigs and leaves clinging to his bushy hair and beard. "I'm Tucker. Tucker the trucker."

Jolene moved closer to Sam, pressing her body against his.

Reaching back, Sam opened the car door for her, but she didn't move. "What are you doing out here, Tucker the trucker, and where's your truck?"

The man laughed, displaying a set of teeth with a few gaps. "I don't have it no more, man. No more truck."

Tucker was missing more than his teeth. "What do you want, Tucker?"

He raised a grubby unsteady finger, pointing over Sam's head. "I live there."

Sam's heart rate ticked up. "You live in that apartment building behind me?"

Tucker nodded, putting the finger to his lips. "I'm not supposed to, but the place is empty. I got in there once, so sometimes I squat there."

"Really?" He must mean the empty apartment right next to Melody's.

"Nobody's there. What's it to you?" Tucker puffed out his scrawny chest.

"Easy, man. I don't care." Sam twisted his head over his shoulder and whispered to Jolene, "Get in the car."

"And miss this? No way." She grabbed the top of the car door, peering over it at Tucker. "Did you know the woman who lived in that apartment? The one where all the cops are?"

"Pinky?" He grinned. "Yeah, I know her. She promised not to tell no one about me living there. She gave me beer sometimes."

"Did you see Pinky tonight, Tucker?" Sam shoved a hand in his pocket. "Did you see what happened?"

Tucker scuffed the toe of his filthy sneaker in the dirt. "Do you have beer?"

"I don't have any beer, but I have some money. If I give you some money, will you tell us what you saw tonight?" Sam pulled a crumpled ten from his pocket and bounced it up and down on his palm in front of Tucker.

When Tucker reached out for it, Sam formed a fist around the bill. "You gotta give me the goods first, Tucker."

"She's dead, huh? Pinky's dead?" The man's nose turned red, and he blinked his watery eyes.

Jolene sniffed. "Yeah, Pinky's dead."

Tucker cackled and slapped the thigh of his raggedy black pants. "I saw who killed her."

Chapter Ten

Jolene's fingers curled around the door, and she caught her breath. She felt like grabbing Tucker and shaking him, but she didn't want to scare him off. The guy seemed ready to blow away with the next breeze.

"You saw what happened to Pinky?"

"I heard." Tucker tapped his head. "I was dreaming in my pad."

"Dreaming?" Sam turned his head and rolled his eyes at her. "You mean you were sleeping?"

"I was sleeping and dreaming." Tucker started combing his fingers through his unkempt beard, not a gray hair visible, but he looked old enough to be Sam's father. "Big loud noise woke me up."

"Did you hear voices?" Sam allowed the ten-dollar bill to peek through his fist, and Tucker's gaze followed every one of Sam's gestures. "Yelling? Screaming?"

"Just a yelp, like a yelp, yip, yap. Big loud noise.

Scraping sound like furniture moving." Tucker narrowed his eyes. "Then he left."

Jolene's heart jumped. "You saw the man who killed Mel… Pinky?"

"I heard footsteps—clomp, bomp, stomp. I eyed, spied though the blinds and saw a man leaving. Stocking cap on his head. It's hot. Nobody needs no stocking cap."

"This rhyming is giving me a headache." Sam rubbed his temple with two fingers. "Did you see what this guy looked like, Tucker? Other than the stocking cap? Beard? Long hair? Clothing?"

Tucker tore at his shirt. "It wasn't me. No beard. It wasn't me. Don't take my thumb, don't take my thumb, don't take my thumb, drum, crumb drive."

"Damn." Sam dragged a hand through his hair. "I didn't say it was you, Tucker, and we're not going to take your thumb. I'm asking what the guy looked like."

"Dark clothes, black clothes. Dark, stark, weird beard." He waved his hands. "Not me, not me. Not my thumb."

"We know that, Tucker." She tugged on Sam's sleeve. "Give him the money for God's sake."

Sam held on to the bill and asked, "Did you see him get into a car? Hear a car?"

"No car. Like me, no truck. But not me." Tucker

started hopping from foot to foot. "It wasn't me. Not my thumb."

Sam smacked a hand against his forehead. "I don't know how much more of this I can take."

Jolene hunched over the car door. "Tucker, can you talk to the police? Tell them what you told us? You want to help Pinky, don't you? She was good to you, and that man hurt her."

"They'll get me for staying in that place when I ain't supposed to. They'll take my thumb drive. Pinky gave me that."

"You're not there now. The cops aren't going to arrest you for anything. They're trying to find out what happened to Pinky." Sam held out the balled up ten to Tucker. "I'll make sure they don't arrest you. Just tell them what you saw."

Tucker snatched the bill and opened his voluminous coat, wet from the rains, to find a place to put the money. As he tugged open one side of his coat, a purse fell to the ground.

Jolene covered her mouth. "Sam, that's Melody's purse."

Tucker made a grab for the purse and shouted, "Not me. Not me. No thumb. In the floor."

He scrambled toward the bushes, and Sam lunged forward and tackled him, pinning his arms behind his back. "That's it, Tucker. Game over. Jolene, go get the police down here."

"Sam!" Jolene clutched her stomach as Tucker

wailed. "You don't really believe he killed Melody, do you?"

"He has her damned purse, Jolene. Go get the cops before I have to hurt him." Sam flipped Tucker over and planted a knee in the middle of the frail man's back.

Jolene jogged across the parking lot and grabbed the first officer she saw. "We ran into a homeless guy near our car. He admitted to squatting in the apartment next to Melody's, and he has her purse."

Another cop overheard her and the two sheriff's deputies hustled toward the edge of the parking lot.

When they arrived, Sam looked up from the squirming Tucker. "I'm Border Patrol. I have my weapon but no cuffs. I didn't have to pull my gun, but you need to take him into custody."

Tucker thrashed on the ground. "You told me you wouldn't call them. Where's my ten bucks? Tucker, trucker. Tucker, trucker."

One of the officers swore. "Oh man, it's Tucker Bishop."

"You know him?" Sam panted. "He's wriggling like a fish on a line over here."

"We pick him up occasionally, mostly for a seventy-two-hour hold in the psych ward. He's usually not violent."

"Yeah, except he's in possession of a dead

woman's purse. He told us he heard someone in Melody's apartment and saw him walk by, but I don't know how much we can trust him."

The deputies approached Sam and Tucker, one of them drawing his weapon. "Stop struggling, Tucker. We're gonna take you to the station and find out what you know, give you a cot and a hot. Why do you have that woman's purse?"

"She gave it to me. She gave me stuff."

Sam finally relinquished control of Tucker to the sheriff's deputies. Standing up, he brushed off his clothing. "I'm going to have to do more laundry."

Jolene spotted Melody's purse on the ground and crouched down, reaching out for it.

"Don't touch it, Jolene. Let them bag it for evidence and test it for prints. The fewer people touching it right now, the better."

She snatched her hand back. "I don't see her phone."

"What?" Sam took a knee beside her.

"Her phone." Jolene poked at the purse with a stick she snatched up from the parking lot. "She'd usually stick it in this side pocket."

Sam pushed to his feet. "Check Tucker's pockets for a phone."

One of the deputies snapped on a pair of gloves and asked Tucker to remove his coat. He searched through the pockets of the coat, and then patted down Tucker.

"Nothing."

Jolene approached Tucker, his hands cuffed behind him, his lips moving with mumbled words. Her heart ached for him. Melody would have been kind to him because Melody had a thing for lost causes.

"Tucker? Did you take Pinky's phone?"

He shook his shaggy head and spittle nestled in his beard. "No phone. No zone. No drone."

"Watch out, Ms. Nighthawk, we're taking him in. We'll ask him about the phone."

As the deputies bagged the purse and hauled off a subdued Tucker, Jolene plopped down in the passenger seat of Sam's car, her legs hanging over the side. "What the heck do you make of that? You can't possibly believe that poor confused man killed Melody."

"You said it. He's confused, Jolene. We don't know what's going on his head. We don't know what drugs he's on. I was willing to play along up until the minute Melody's purse fell out of his coat. He could've heard her come home, gone next door, asked for a beer. Maybe Melody invited him in, he saw her purse and decided to take it. She fought back, fell and hit her head." He shrugged in a way that encompassed everything else.

Jolene pinned her hands between her knees. "I don't know. If Tucker did kill her, why did he accost us in the parking lot? We didn't know he was there. He could've disappeared with Melody's purse. Nobody would've known of his presence. The cops might not have even discovered that he'd been in the apartment next door. Why implicate himself when he didn't have to?"

"Really, Jolene?" Sam raised his eyebrows. "You're acting like Tucker the trucker is a reasonable, rational human being, instead of a drug-and-booze-addled vagrant."

She dropped her head to her knees. "Oh, Melody, why'd you start drinking again?"

Sam stroked her hair. "I'm going to get you home—before something else happens."

When Sam got behind the wheel, Jolene tapped his forearm. "Is Melody Nighthawk going to be another person in that death register whose death is marked down as accidental? We need to comb through those names."

"Not tonight. Do you need to call someone, Granny Viv, or will Wade take care of that?" He plucked a charger from the cup holder. "I don't think this will work with your phone."

"Wade will tell Gran. I'll charge my phone when I get home." She ran a finger down the thigh of his jeans. "Do you have to go back to your motel? I—I'm still rattled after everything that went on today. I'd rather not be alone—even with Chip there."

"I had no intention of leaving you alone to-night."

Jolene eased out a sigh and slumped in the seat. Was she inviting trouble by asking Sam to stay? Could she have him in her home and not her bed?

She'd find out soon enough.

WHEN HE WALKED into her house, Sam removed his weapon from his waistband and set it on the kitchen table. He pinched his T-shirt between two fingers and pulled it away from his body. "Every time I step into your home, there's something wrong with my clothes."

Jolene searched the counter for her phone charger. "What is it this time?"

"Did you get a look at Tucker and his clothing? He and it weren't too clean, and I had to tackle the guy." He pulled his T-shirt up to his face and sniffed it. "Yeah, this definitely has to go in the wash."

"I should start charging you for laundry." Jolene walked to her bedroom and plugged her phone into the charger on her nightstand.

When she returned to the living room, Chip had joined in on the sniffing. His nose was twitching as he checked out Sam's jeans.

"Even Chip notices." Sam patted the dog's head. "Good boy."

Jolene dropped onto the couch. "I can't believe Melody is dead. Gran is going to be heartbroken."

"Should you call her? You can use my phone again."

"I'll let Wade handle it. He might not even want to wake her at this hour to give her the news. We'll see her tomorrow." Tears pricked the back of Jolene's eyes, and she covered her face.

Sam rubbed a circle on her back. "I wish I had confronted her about drinking when she waved us down. I didn't want to get in her face, you know?"

"I know, and I feel like we could've gotten to the bar faster." She dropped her hands. "Was cleaning the kitchen so important? Changing clothes?"

"We didn't know what was going to happen, Jolene. Who could predict how this night would end?"

"Did she seem scared to you earlier? She did warn me."

"If she was so frightened, she wouldn't have gone out drinking on her own. She would've stayed at her brother's place, his gated home with the security system. Wade could've kept her safe if she was afraid."

"Unless she was afraid of Wade." She twisted

her head around and met Sam's blue eyes. "Why are you hovering back there? Have a seat."

He thumped a hand against his chest. "You don't wanna get too close to this. I'm going to shower and put on those sweats I dug out of your closet earlier. Is that okay with you?"

"Go ahead. Do you want some tea, coffee, water?"

"I don't need anything to keep me awake. I'm already wired. You?" He yanked the T-shirt over his head, and she gulped.

She had the same visceral reaction she'd always had to the sight of Sam Cross's body—tingling excitement now mixed with an ache of longing.

"Same." She pushed up from the couch, trying to put distance between her and Sam's bare chest. "I'm going to make myself a cup of herbal tea. I'll make you one, too. You want it. You just don't know you want it yet."

"If it can help with the pounding in my head that was going on before we were subjected to Tucker the trucker and then got worse when I talked to him, I'm all for it." He pointed to the hallway. "Clean towel in the linen closet?"

"Help yourself, and you can stuff your clothes in the washer while you're at it."

She banged around in the kitchen, pulling tea bags and mugs from the cupboards, while Sam banged around in the hall closet. She hoped he wouldn't follow her instructions literally, and take off all his clothes and put them in the wash before he got in the shower. Sam shirtless had already tested her defenses. Sam naked would bring her walls crumbling down around her.

Jolene let out a long breath when she heard the water in the shower. She filled the mugs with water and stuck them in the microwave.

Two minutes later, she dredged the tea bags in the boiling water of each cup. If Sam didn't want the tea, she'd have a second cup.

She hunched over the counter, burying her chin in her palm. How had everything gotten so complicated? She'd planned to dump the bones she'd gotten from her friend in the U of A archaeology department at the construction site to muck up the work over there and do a little more digging into her father's death. How had it ended in Melody's death?

Of course, Melody could've been doing her own snooping that led to her death. Or maybe she'd taken a tumble and hit her head all by herself. She and Tucker could've gotten into a tug-of-war over the purse.

Sam stepped into the kitchen dressed in nothing but those Border Patrol sweats again, droplets of water shimmering on his chest, his clothes bunched in one hand. "Do you have anything you want to put in with these?"

At least the sweats seemed to be pulled up higher on his waist.

Chip trotted into the kitchen, his claws tapping on the tile floor. Sam bent over to scratch Chip behind the ear, and the sweats dipped a little more.

"No, knock yourself out. I have a short cycle, though, so you should use that to save water." She cleared her throat and held up one of the steaming mugs. "Tea?"

"I'll give it a try." He disappeared into the laundry room off the kitchen and turned on the washing machine with several beeps.

When he came out, she handed him a cup of tea. "That sounded like way too many beeps for the short cycle."

"I had to make a few corrections." He held the mug under his nose and closed his eyes. "It smells good, anyway, but most tea tastes like slightly flavored hot water to me."

She pushed at his back, his skin smooth beneath her fingertips. "It's soothing. Give it a try. Do you want some ibuprofen for your head?"

"That warm shower did the trick." He wrapped one hand around the mug and tilted his head, a damp lock of hair curling over his forehead. "How do you feel? It seems days instead of hours ago that I ran a bath for you to relax after your accident. How are those bruises on your arms? Your neck?"

She ran a hand across the back of her neck. "My neck's a little stiff, but I'm okay. Bruises are coloring up nicely. I just wish I could dial back the clock to the moment when Melody ran out to the street to warn me."

"Me, too, but that's futile. Believe me, I've wanted to turn the clock back many times." He touched his mug to hers. "Let's sit down and drink our tea—never thought I'd hear myself saying that. C'mon, Chip."

"You might like it." She strolled into the living room with Sam right behind her and Chip right behind him, his devoted follower. She sat on one side of the couch, grabbed the remote and turned on the TV. She didn't want any awkward silences between them.

Sam took the cushion next to her and noisily slurped his tea. "Yep, flavored hot water, but it's kind of minty."

She aimed the remote at the TV. "Have you seen this show?"

"Heard about it, haven't seen it." He stretched his arm across her shoulders and pulled her close. "It's okay now. Everything's going to be okay."

"But Melody..." She rested her head on his shoulder. Maybe she didn't want to put her trust in Sam for the long term, but for right now he represented something solid.

"I know." He smoothed the hair back from her forehead, his fingers tickling her skin.

Chip curled up on her feet, and Sam ran the sole of his foot across Chip's back. "See? Chip's here for you, too. We both are."

Jolene took another sip of her tea and set the cup on the coffee table. She turned to Sam and cupped his lean jaw in her hand. "I don't know what I want from you, Sam—maybe nothing. Maybe you're not prepared to offer anything."

He opened his mouth, and she put a finger to his lips. "But right now, I need you."

She replaced her finger with her lips, kissing his mint-flavored mouth.

He slipped his arms around her and deepened their kiss, his hands sliding down her back. He murmured against her mouth, "I love you, Jolene. I never stopped loving you."

"Don't." She skimmed her hands across his shoulders, and then dug her fingernails into his flesh. "You don't have to tell me anything right now. You don't have to convince me of anything. I just want to be with you. Can we do that? Just be?"

He cinched his hands around her waist and pulled her into his lap so that she straddled him. "We can do whatever you want. I'm yours."

His words caused a thrill to race down her spine. Her fingertips buzzed, and she trailed them over the sculpted muscles of his chest, circling one brown nipple before she kissed it. She ran a finger along the waistband of the sweats.

"Easy on, easy off. How convenient." She tugged at the sweats, discovering Sam had stripped off his underwear, too. "*Very* convenient."

"I aim to please." He nuzzled her throat, planting a line of kisses on her shoulder. Then he peeled her T-shirt from her body, as she lifted her arms.

"I aim to please, too."

"You don't have to do anything to please me." He fumbled with her bra. "Except take this off."

She obliged and threw the undergarment over her head.

Chip scrambled to his feet and went to investigate.

"He's not going to chew that up, is he?" Sam had stopped caressing her breast as he eyed Chip across the room.

"Don't worry about him." She tried yanking down the sweats, but she was still sitting on Sam's lap and didn't get very far. "Should we take this into the bedroom...away from the watching eyes of Chip?"

"Definitely."

He scooped her up in his arms, both of them topless now, and she pressed her bare skin against his. She'd missed the feel of him.

He carried her into the bedroom and kicked the door closed behind them. "In case Chip gets any ideas."

She slid off his body and stood on her tiptoes, as he kissed her by the side of the bed, one hand placed at the back of her head. She didn't even mind the slight shaft of pain that needled her neck.

Her fingers slipped into the waistband of the sweats and tugged them down over the curve of his backside. Her hands kneaded his muscled buttocks, which he flexed for her benefit. "Someone's been running."

He stepped out of the sweats and kicked them across the floor. Then he reached for the button on her jeans.

"Wait." She grabbed his hand and, placing the palm of her other hand against his chest, she pushed him back a few steps. "I want to see what I've been missing these past few years."

Always the goofball, Sam folded his hands behind his head and posed, his erection on full display. The glow from the moon coming through the window played across the planes and bulges of his body.

"Is there enough light in here for you to get the

full effect of my manliness? All we have is your charging phone and the moon."

She snorted and slid a hand along his shaft. "I couldn't miss this with a night-light."

As she caressed him, he closed his eyes and caught his breath. "Your hands feel like silk, but you know what I really miss?"

She dragged her nails down his chest. "This?"

He gasped. "No."

She knelt before him and ran her tongue along the length of him. "This?"

"Oh." His body shuddered. "No."

She took him in her mouth, sucking him hard, her own pleasure heating her blood. When she finished, she looked up. "That?"

He growled. "All of it, but what I really miss is how you used to trail your hair down my body. I can fantasize about that in the middle of the day, and it never fails to make me hard."

"Must make chasing bad guys a little...hard." She smirked at her joke.

He fell across the bed. "Come here and make my fantasies come true."

Crouching beside him, she whipped her hair back and forth, and then proceeded to lean over him, the ends of her hair tickling his flesh. "Like this?"

"It's even better than I remember, but why do

you still have your jeans on?" He unbuttoned her fly and yanked down the zipper.

In one move, he swept her onto her back and pulled her pants and underwear off the rest of the way.

His eyes gleamed in the semidarkness. "You're right. There's plenty of light in here to see all the good stuff."

Nudging her legs apart, he kneeled between them. He bent over her and took possession of her mouth, kissing her hard. He skimmed his hand over the top of his head. "I'd run my hair over your body, but I think it'd be prickly instead of sensuous. I do have other tricks at my disposal, though."

"Did you always talk this much during sex?" She rubbed her hands against the flared muscles of his thighs.

"Must be nerves." He took one of her nipples between his lips and suckled her, as his fingers moved between her legs.

He played with her throbbing folds just enough to get her squirming. Then he switched his attentions to her other peaked nipple.

She sucked in a breath and lifted her hips from the bed. She gritted her teeth and said, "You know what my fantasy has been since the minute I laid eyes on you in the desert?"

He stopped teasing her breast, but his fingers

kept toying with her. Resting his scruffy chin on her chest, he said, "What?"

"You, inside of me."

"Like this?" He shoved two fingers into her core.

She thrashed her head to the side and bit her lip. "While that's nice…"

"Nice?" With his fingers still inside her, he dragged his thumb across her swollen flesh.

A low moan wrenched from her throat. "More than nice, but I want that other part of your anatomy inside me. You know, the bigger part."

His lips twisted and before she even had time to prepare herself for the onslaught, he plowed into her.

She clawed at his back. Already driven to the pinnacle by his touch, she held her breath as he thrust against her once, twice, three times.

Her toes curled and all her muscles coiled the second before the first wave of passion coursed through her body. Other waves followed, each a little less intense than that first crash, each flooding her with warmth.

Before she got too relaxed, Sam's body stiffened and in a hoarse voice, he demanded, "Open your eyes."

Her lids flew open to meet his intense blue gaze. He stared right into her soul as he came inside her. As his body shuddered, he bent his head and kissed her mouth, just a gentle touch of his lips.

Still connected to her, Sam dug an elbow into the pillow next to her head and braced his chin against his palm. "Did your fantasy go something like that?"

She screwed up her mouth and rolled her eyes to the ceiling. "*Something* like that. I think we'll have to try again later to see if we can get closer."

He rolled off her body and nestled his front against her side, draping one heavy leg over her hip. "You've gotten demanding over the years."

Pinching his chin, she said, "My resolve went right out the window the minute I saw you in those sweats this afternoon."

"What resolve was that?" He sucked her thumb into his mouth while he cupped her mound.

"You're doing it again." But she didn't pull away. She wriggled in even closer to him so that his fingers dipped between her legs.

He scraped his nails against the flesh of her inner thighs. "I can always stop."

"Don't you dare." She climbed on top of him, straddling his hips.

The light from her phone, charging on her nightstand, drew her gaze. "Oh, God. It looks like I have texts. I hope Wade didn't wake up Gran to tell her about Melody. Her nerves don't need that."

He patted her bottom. "Go ahead and look. I'm going to hit the bathroom."

Reluctantly, she slid from his body, and then a twinge of guilt needled her brain. Her cousin had died tonight and here she was rolling in the sheets with Sam.

As Sam clambered from the bed and staggered to the bathroom door, the sheets twisted around his ankles, Jolene curled her legs beneath her and snatched her phone from the charger. Drawing her brows together, she tapped the first text and blood pounded against her temples.

"Sam! Sam!" She brought the phone close to her face, the words from the text swimming in front of her eyes.

"What's wrong?" He came charging out of the bathroom, his hair wild, his eyes wide.

She held out her phone to face him. "I got a message from Melody."

Chapter Eleven

Sam rushed toward the bed, tripping on the sheets and kicking them out of the way, adrenaline pumping through his system.

He dropped onto the bed and grabbed the phone from her. "What do you mean? From Melody or her phone? What does it say?"

"It's nonsense. The text says *El Gringo Viejo*."

Sam's blood ran cold in his veins as he stared at the phone's display, unable to see the text. And now he *had* to see this text.

He handed the phone back to Jolene. "You must've clicked off the text when you gave the phone to me. Get it back. When was it sent? Did she send it or did the person who took her phone send it?"

Jolene covered her mouth. "I don't know. I didn't look."

She swept her thumb across the screen. "The text was sent two minutes after midnight. What time did we get to the Sundowner?"

"We were there around midnight. She'd already left, gotten a ride from someone. You'd called her by that time, but she didn't answer. The next time you tried calling, your phone had died. She must've sent you that text when your phone was dead."

Jolene threw the phone into the jumbled bed covers. "If my phone hadn't died, we might've been able to help her."

"Maybe not, Jolene." Sam retrieved the phone to make sure she'd read the text correctly. "She wasn't asking for help, was she?"

"No, but at least she'd contacted me."

He read the words on the display disbelievingly. "You're right. She texted *El Gringo Viejo*."

"What the hell does that mean? Old white guy?" She dug her hands into her hair. "Do you think that's who killed her? Some old white guy? Why would she text that in Spanish?"

"Jolene—" Sam cupped the phone between his hands "—El Gringo Viejo is a drug supplier in Mexico."

"What?" She collapsed against the headboard and rubbed the back of her head after banging it. "Why would Melody text that? What does that even mean? How would she know this man?"

"She must've known something about him, something about his dealings on this side of the border." Sam scratched his chin. "I don't get why his name is even coming up. Last month, we were able to finally identify him. Turns out, he's a guy named Ted Jessup. We got his prints and everything, found out he'd been holing up in Rocky Point."

"Rocky Point?"

His eyes must've been wandering, as she dragged a pillow into her lap to cover up all the good naked parts.

"I'd hardly call that holing up. Rocky Point is a tourist destination."

"The point is, nobody knew what he was doing there. He was just another rich gringo with a villa in the cliffs overlooking the sea. Then a couple of people made him, and the FBI was able to descend on his place—but he'd already escaped."

"He must be back in business." She flicked her fingers at him. "Could you put some clothes on? All this is distracting as hell."

He crawled over her legs to reach over the side of the bed and swipe up his sweats.

She wiggled her toes beneath the weight of him. "That's not helping."

He plumped a pillow against the headboard and flopped down next to her, pulling up the sweats. "Is that better?"

Glancing at the soft material covering his crotch and visible lump there, she said, "Marginally."

"I can't help it." He plucked at the sweats to hide his erection. "You're still naked."

"Is that all it takes to set you off? A naked woman with a pillow in her lap?" She crawled to the foot of the bed to retrieve her underwear, and he reclined against the pillow to enjoy the view.

"Is this a test?" He swept his hand over the curve of her derriere, her skin like silk beneath his fingertips. "Because you're flashing me, and no man in his right mind could resist that."

"Can we get back to the subject at hand?" She snatched up her panties and wriggled into them, clutching the pillow to her chest. "Why would Melody text me this man's moniker? She was warning us about looking into the casino project. Do you think this El Gringo Viejo could have anything to do with it?"

"Come back up here." He patted the mattress next to him. "I promise I'll keep my hands to myself and stay on topic."

She joined him, unfurling her long legs in front of her, twisting her hair behind her head into a bun. "Could he be involved?"

Sam crossed his hands behind his head to keep them off Jolene's body and took a deep breath. He'd been drunk on making love with her, and even though Melody's text had sobered him up, Jolene's nearness was more intoxicating than a sip of Chivas.

He closed his eyes, his mind running over his case. The people they'd discovered dead and buried in the desert near San Diego had all died from a single shot to the head—execution style, drug-cartel style, even though their heads were still attached to their bodies. Their deaths had coincided with the appearance of a pure form of meth flooding the streets of southern California, pink meth.

That same meth had made its appearance in Arizona and New Mexico about four years ago—at the same time, a spate of missing persons had been reported in the area. Could El Gringo Viejo be behind the production and distribution of that meth?

He'd been active in Arizona for a number of years—not so much in California, but the appearance of the potent meth in Cali probably coincided with EGV feeling the heat in Rocky Point. Maybe he expanded his business to get out of Arizona where it had gotten too hot for him.

"What are you doing?" Jolene poked his ribs. "Are you sleeping?"

He grabbed her finger and kissed the tip. "I'm thinking."

"Are you going to let me in on your thoughts or does just talking to me about any subject in bed turn you on?"

Opening one eye, he turned his head. "Yeah, that's pretty much it, and you're still topless."

"I'm hugging a pillow."

"Lucky pillow."

She hit him over the head with the pillow and scrambled from the bed. She threw open her closet door, grabbing the first thing in front of her and pulling it on. Then she jumped back on the bed, the loose-fitting blouse floating around her.

"Better?"

His gaze raked her top half and the way the blouse settled around the curve of her breasts, her dusky nipple visible through the light material. "Yep, that's it, totally turned off."

Truth was, Jolene could wear a burlap sack and they could be discussing the national debt, and he wouldn't be totally immune to her charms and the sexual tension that buzzed between them like a living thing—and she knew it.

A rosy blush seeped into her cheeks, as she crossed her legs beneath her. "Okay, let me in on your thoughts about this character."

He gathered his wits again, and explained the connection between the bodies and the powerful meth hitting the streets. "We had the same occurrence in Arizona about four years back, before I was assigned to this sector but I read all about it. When that meth surfaced in San Diego and it coincided with our discovery of a dumping ground for drug couriers, I remembered what happened in Paradiso. Only difference is, we never found the bodies here."

"Do you think El Gringo Viejo could be responsible for that meth?" She pinned her knees to her chest, wrapping her arms around her legs.

"Border Patrol, FBI and DEA thought so at the time, but they could never pin it on him. He's always been more of a facilitator between the cartels and the suppliers. He wouldn't want the cartels to know he was selling and encroaching on their business."

"And you think the dumping ground here for those bodies could be the Desert Sun Casino construction site."

"It's similar to the other location in California in many ways. That's why I went out there the night I ran into you. I'd been looking at a map of the desert, and that site jumped out at me."

"We need to search that land, Sam." She rested her chin on her knees. "Now it's not just my father's death I have to investigate, it's Melody's."

"That's what law enforcement is for." Even as the words left his mouth, he knew Jolene would never accept them.

A light kindled in her dark eyes. "You don't even have enough proof to justify a search of the land. What chance do I have to convince anyone? That's why I buried those bones out there. I may be found out soon, but that discovery caused enough of a delay to buy us some time."

"I'd planned to do the search on my own." He swung his legs over the side of the bed and launched forward to collect the mess of sheets on the floor.

"You wouldn't even have had the opportunity to get on that property if it hadn't been for my scheme." She yanked on the edge of the top sheet as he handed it to her and smoothed it across the bed. "You owe me."

"Okay, we'll go out there together, but it has to be at night." He tucked the edge of the sheet under the mattress. "Now let's get some sleep before the sun comes up."

"I'm dreading the day ahead. Gran is going to be devastated by Melody's death. Do you think Tucker confessed yet?"

"So, now you think he did it?"

"Of course not, but that doesn't mean the poor soul isn't going to confess to it." She rolled out of bed. "I need to brush my teeth…and stuff. Do you want a toothbrush?"

He tapped his front tooth. "Before you got that text, I was in the bathroom rubbing toothpaste over my teeth with my finger."

"I have extra toothbrushes. You could've asked." She padded to the bathroom, looking sexy as hell with that blouse floating around her.

While she ran the water in the bathroom, he straightened the covers on the bed.

"Here you go." She tossed him an unwrapped toothbrush as she exited the bathroom, and then pulled the bedroom curtains tight, shrouding the room in darkness.

He brushed his teeth and left the new toothbrush on the edge of the sink. Should he read anything into the toothbrush?

She'd already admitted to him she didn't know if she could trust him for the long haul. He'd have to change her mind. In the meantime, the short haul had been deeply satisfying.

He crept into the bedroom to find Jolene under the covers, one bare shoulder visible. At least she'd gotten rid of the blouse. He stripped off his sweats and crawled into bed naked, nestling up to her back. She'd left her underwear in place.

She reached behind him and skimmed her knuckles down his hip. "What happened to your clothes?"

"I only put those on so we could think." He wrapped an arm around her body and cupped her breast, dragging his thumb across her nipple while the breath hitched in her throat. "We don't have to think anymore, do we?"

She turned around within his embrace, and pressed her lips to his. She murmured against his mouth, "If I thought about what I was doing, I might stop."

And as he didn't want to think about what she had just said, he thrust his erection against her belly and proceeded to make her his own...while he still could.

THE NEXT MORNING, Sam carefully extricated himself from Jolene's limbs tangled with his. Before he slipped out of bed, he paused to study her face. A small bruise had formed over her left eyebrow, and her bottom lip looked slightly swollen—of course that could be from all the kisses they'd shared. He couldn't get enough of her.

He tiptoed from her bedroom and into the laundry room where he retrieved yesterday's clothes from the dryer. He got dressed in the living room, and set about making coffee.

He checked his own phone charging on the kitchen counter—a few texts from Aimee's mother about Jess and a call from work, but nothing as dramatic as Jolene's text last night. If only Melody could've given them more than El Gringo Viejo's name. Maybe she didn't know anything more about him—or maybe she was too drunk to know what she was doing.

The coffee started to drip in the pot, and he raided Jolene's fridge for eggs, butter, milk, cheese and a leftover pepper and onion. Since the separation from Aimee—the second separation—he'd gotten pretty good in the kitchen.

As the first omelet bubbled in the frying pan, Jolene scuffed into the kitchen, the blouse from last night hanging off her, the first several buttons undone. "Smells good, but it's lunchtime. I slept so late."

"You were in a car accident yesterday. I think you deserved to sleep late." He jiggled the pan. "I'm making omelets."

"I'm impressed." She yawned. "But my accident is not the reason why I slept late. I think that had something to do with the man in my bed."

"At least I'm properly dressed now, which is more than I can say for you." He waved the spatula at her. "Whoever told you that was a modest blouse was lying, especially when it's open to your navel."

She clutched the top of the blouse and yanked the two pieces together. "I'll go take a shower and get dressed. Don't get any ideas about joining me in the shower. I'm sore."

He wiggled his eyebrows up and down. "I'm that good, huh?"

She picked up a balled-up paper towel from the counter and fired it at him. "My muscles are sore from the accident. Look at my arms."

He eyed the bruises from the airbag on her

arms. "I saw those, but that airbag probably cut down on the damage to the rest of your body."

"I suppose so." She wrapped her hair around one hand. "I already have a million calls from Gran and Wade and everyone else this morning, so I guess what happened to Melody was not a bad dream."

"I'm sorry it wasn't." He slid the first omelet onto a plate. "Any chance you can get into Melody's apartment today?"

"What do you mean? Isn't it a crime scene? The sheriff's department arrested Tucker yesterday. They already had the crime scene tape up before we left last night."

"You stole onto a construction site and planted some bones. You can't figure out how to get past a little crime scene tape and into your cousin's apartment?"

"You're encouraging me to break the law, Agent Cross?" She folded her arms and tapped a bare foot on the floor.

"You need encouragement?" He cracked two more eggs into the bowl. "Go get dressed, and I'll finish breakfast."

"If you think we might find something useful at Melody's, I'll get in there. I have to see Gran and the rest of the family first. Do you think you can find out what's happening with Tucker?"

"Yeah, I'll do that."

Jolene slipped out of the kitchen, and a few minutes later, he heard the shower running. He'd have liked nothing more than to join her, but she needed sustenance and painkillers right now—not another tumble in the sheets.

He finished cooking the second omelet, shoved some bread in the toaster and poured himself a cup of coffee. He even set the table and fed Chip.

When he looked up from placing the silverware next to the plates of food, Jolene was studying him, one hand on her hip. "You've become quite domestic."

"Now that I have Jess on my own, my apartment is immaculate."

One corner of her mouth lifted. "Never thought I'd see the day. I—I'd like to see you with your daughter someday."

"She's funny right now—and bossy." Should he be bragging to Jolene about Jess? He wanted to share his daughter with Jolene, but it hurt him that Jess wasn't hers.

"It's a cute age—which I know from my cousins' kids." She grabbed the back of a chair and sat down, picking up a fork. "I know where Melody hid a key to her place, so if the cops aren't watching her apartment, I can get in. How long will they designate it as an active crime scene?"

He shrugged and took a seat at the table. "Depends on what Tucker's been telling them. They were already searching her place. May have taken her computer and other electronic devices."

"I wonder if they found her phone? She must've texted me on her way home. I wish she would've told me how she was getting there." She wrapped both hands around her coffee mug and stared into the cup.

"Maybe she thought she was in the app car." Sam sawed into his omelet and stabbed at the piece of egg with his fork. "She called for a car, she was drunk and didn't realize she was getting into some random car. It's happened before."

"You mean someone was waiting for her. Knew she'd called for a car and took advantage of her inebriated state." She took a sip of coffee. "We need to talk to Eddie, the bartender. Maybe he saw someone hanging around her."

"We still need a motive. Tucker has a motive. He had her purse. He also had opportunity and the means."

"Do you really think that scrawny guy could've overpowered Melody?" She plunged her fork into the omelet and raised it to her mouth, a string of cheese hanging off the end.

"She was drunk, Jolene. Wasted, according to Eddie—and he should know. Maybe she did hit her head on the edge of that table while she was struggling with Tucker. She pulled away from him and fell. Tucker wouldn't have had to do anything."

"Why are you trying to convict Tucker? I thought you were going with the fake driver story." She dragged a paper towel across her mouth, but the cheese clung to her chin.

Sam reached over and dislodged the cheese with a dab of his finger against her face. "I'm playing devil's advocate. Tucker's motive was robbery. The fake driver's motive could've been knowledge."

"You mean Melody knew too much. Maybe part of what she knew was that El Gringo Viejo was involved in the casino project...and maybe some deaths connected to the project."

"Could be, but why didn't she go to the police? She could've laid out everything she knew for them and gotten some protection. A woman one of our agents is dating knows too much about El Gringo Viejo and she's under protection."

Her eyes widened. "Rob Valdez's girlfriend? That woman who showed up in Paradiso with amnesia?"

"That's the one, Libby James." He put his fork to his lips. "But you're not supposed to know that. It's life and death for her. Do you understand?"

"Of course. Didn't my cousin just get killed for the same reason?" She crunched into her toast and a shower of crumbs rained down on her plate.

"You came to that conclusion quickly. We were still discussing Tucker's guilt."

"I just don't believe it. I know you law enforcement types have to go with the evidence instead of feelings, but the cops don't know what we know about Melody and the casino project." She dusted her fingers together. "Should we tell them?"

"Not yet." Sam shook his head. "I can't believe I'm saying this, but I don't want to tell them until I have a chance to search that construction site. You talk about feelings over evidence? I've had a hunch about the connection between the missing people here and the bodies we found east of San Diego for over a month now, but I can't get a search warrant for that property based on my hunches. Doesn't work that way."

"So, you're going rogue. I like it."

"And the food? Do you like the food?" He aimed his fork at her half-eaten omelet.

"It's hard to talk and eat at the same time. It's great. Even Chip wants some." She nudged Chip with her foot. "You got dressed without taking a shower. Do you want to shower here? I have to get over to Gran's."

"I'll clean up at the motel. I need to go into the station, and that means I need my uniform. Besides…" he ran a thumb across her bottom lip "…I still have the scent of you on my skin."

"If you need to get to the station, and I definitely need to go to Gran's house, you'd better stop saying things like that." She pressed her lips together. "I'll clean up since you cooked."

"I'll let Chip out again. Should I leave the dog door open?" He strode to the sliding doors that led to the back, whistling for Chip.

Jolene picked up his cell phone. "Your phone's ringing. It's the station."

Sam slid open the door to set Chip free, and then turned to grab his phone from Jolene. "Cross here."

"It's Clay."

"Hey, Clay. What can I do for you? I was planning to come in this morning."

"This is really just a courtesy call, Sam. You know that transient who was arrested for having Melody's purse? The guy you held for the police?"

Sam's mouth got dry, and his pulse drummed in his ears."

"Yeah? What about him?"

"He's dead."

Chapter Twelve

Jolene furrowed her brow as she watched Sam clutching the phone with white knuckles, his chest heaving.

She whispered, "What about who?"

Same held up a finger at her. "How the hell did that happen, Clay?"

He paused, but whatever Clay was telling him was winding him up even more, as two red spots formed on his cheeks and lights flared in his blue eyes. "That's negligent. That's criminal. What did he say during questioning?"

Jolene twisted her fingers in front of her. Were they discussing Tucker? Had he confessed?

"This is unbelievable. They're gonna have to do a full investigation and heads should roll." His jaw tightened and Jolene could almost hear the teeth grinding from the kitchen. "Yeah, yeah."

He ended the call and held the phone in his hand, staring at it.

"What is it? What happened?"

Shoving the phone in his back pocket, he joined her in the kitchen. He put his hand on her arm and now her heart was galloping.

"Tucker Bishop killed himself in his jail cell this morning."

Her knees weakened and she grabbed the edge of the counter. "How?"

"He hung himself with the bedsheets." Sam tossed the leftover coffee from his cup into the sink and brown liquid marred the spotless porcelain. "How the hell did the deputies allow that to happen?"

"D-did he confess to murdering Melody before he killed himself?"

"No. He wouldn't cough up anything. Seems he told them less than he revealed to us. We probably know more than the police do about what Tucker was doing there and what he saw and heard." He cranked on the faucet and rinsed down the sink— busy work for agitated hands.

"Now we're not going to learn any more of what Tucker knew." She pressed a hand to her face. "Sam, do you think someone got to Tucker in jail? Does that kind of thing happen?"

He hunched over the sink, his T-shirt clinging to his tightly coiled muscles. "That stuff happens all the time, especially if the guy wasn't on suicide watch."

"Would Tucker have been on suicide watch?"

"Not unless he made statements that would indicate he was suicidal, which I guess he didn't."

"That's ridiculous. The man was obviously not in his right mind. Wouldn't that be considered suicidal on its surface?"

"Doesn't work that way. He didn't even confess to harming Melody."

"Because he didn't." Jolene folded her arms over her stomach. "But he knew who did, and that's why he was silenced."

"Whoa!" Sam spun around. "You're jumping fast and hard to some serious conclusions."

"C'mon, Sam. That's exactly what you're thinking. I saw it on your face when you were talking to Clay on the phone."

He plowed a hand through his hair. "What you're suggesting would require several things to happen—none of them complimentary to the Pima County Sheriff's Department."

"I'm not saying a deputy murdered Tucker, but you know how he was—highly unstable."

"That's an understatement."

"It wouldn't have taken much to drive that poor man over the edge completely—haranguing, suggestions, lies."

"You're implying someone was paid off to take him over that edge?" He rubbed his chin. "If so, we're in trouble. I'm going to have to be careful about my interest in the construction site, and the sooner I have a look, the better."

"The sooner *we* have a look, the better. There's no way you're keeping me away from that land."

Sam opened his mouth and then snapped it shut when he took in Jolene's flaring nostrils and the martial light in her eyes. When she got that look, nobody could tell her anything.

She wore that same look when he'd told her about his ex's pregnancy, and she'd ordered him to go back to his wife and unborn child and to forget about her...as if that were ever going to happen.

AT THE END of the day, Jolene collapsed on her couch, drained and depressed. Not even Chip licking at her hand could bring a smile to her face.

Chip had already been hard at work trying to cheer people up, as she'd brought him to Gran's house where the family had met to mourn Melody and discuss arrangements. All the relatives believed it was a robbery gone wrong with Tucker Bishop as the culprit. His suicide in jail had confirmed their beliefs.

Who was she to dissuade them? It had brought them a measure of comfort on a dark day.

As Sam had mentioned, they needed to keep a low profile regarding their suspicions about the casino project and what Melody may or may not have known about it. They didn't want to alert anyone to their interest any more than she'd already done so via her stunt with the bones.

And if those bones came back to her, it could all be dismissed as her concern for the land as a Yaqui.

She plucked at her skirt. She should probably change before Sam got here. He was coming over with dinner, and then they were heading to the construction site to have a look around.

Instead, she closed her eyes and patted Chip's head as he rested it against her knee. Two seconds later, a knock on the door made her jerk upright.

Chip whined and scampered to the front door. If he wasn't barking, he must know Sam was on the other side of that door. She glanced at her phone and jumped up from the couch. She'd been asleep for almost an hour.

She peeked through the blinds at Sam holding bags of food. Nudging Chip aside with her foot, she cracked open the door. "Come on in. I fell asleep on the couch."

"Get back, Chip." Sam pushed his way past the excited dog. "Chinese, is that okay?"

"I could've cooked something." She closed and locked the door, and then took a plastic bag twisted around Sam's fingers.

"You must've had a rough day if you fell asleep on the couch." He placed his bag on the counter. "How'd it go with the family? How's Granny Viv?"

"Heartbroken."

"It must've been a hard day for everyone." He reached for a couple of plates from the cupboard. "Are you sure you want to come with me tonight?"

"Oh, no you don't." She waved a fork at him. "Don't try to dissuade me. I'm coming with you. I know where my father's body was found, and that's where we're going to start. It's a big piece of property. You can't just wander around in the dark, staring at the ground."

"I don't know what I expect to find there. Hasn't all that land been prepped for the construction? Isn't that why Wade knew there was something fishy about those bones?" He dipped into one of the bags and pulled out a carton of rice.

"Yeah, that was an amateur move on my part, but I had to put those bones where they'd be discovered during the ground-breaking ceremony." She plunged a couple of spoons into the other containers. "There's a part of that land that hasn't been prepared yet, though. They're holding that aside for a golf course, or something like that. Can you imagine green grass out there, and the amount of water it would take to keep it that way?"

"Other resorts out here have golf courses."

"Oh, so this is a resort now? Wade won't stop until he's built up a theme park for the whole family—Yaqui World."

Sam snorted. "I doubt that. So, there's untouched land bordering the construction area?"

"Yeah, and you need me to find it. So, don't get any ideas about leaving me out." She carried the food to the kitchen table. "We could eat this in the living room, but Chip would be all over us."

"Kitchen table is good."

They settled at the table with the open cartons of food in front of them and Chip at their feet.

"The whole family believes Tucker Bishop killed Melody to steal her purse. Did you learn anything more about his suicide?"

"I did." Sam scooted the peppers from his kung pao into a little pile on the edge of his plate. "The security camera in the jail cell isn't working."

Jolene dropped her chopsticks, flicking grains of rice into the air. "You're kidding."

"I wish I were. The deputies checked the security footage for that row of cells, and all they saw was fuzz. There was some trouble with that camera before, which makes the malfunction slightly more believable. But why put prisoners in those cells when you've already had issues with the cameras? It's not like there was no room in the cells."

"This stinks, Sam. It sounds like someone was

on the take, ordered to keep Tucker quiet one way or the other."

"It's not my department. I can't order an investigation." He picked up a piece of chicken with his chopsticks, but it fell back to his plate before he could get it into his mouth. "Problem is, Tucker was a transient. He doesn't have anyone to demand that investigation."

"That's just sad." She held out a fork to him. "I can't stand to watch you anymore. You're going to starve using those chopsticks."

"I got this." He balanced the same piece of chicken on the ends of the chopsticks and hurried it into his mouth. "Did you get a chance to visit Melody's apartment?"

"No time, but I set myself up to go in there by offering to pack up her things. I can probably get in there legally instead of trying to sneak in, don't you think?"

"The sheriffs will probably let you in even if the yellow tape is still up. It might still be designated a crime scene, but it's most likely no longer active. They've ransacked the place by now—dusted for prints, collected blood and other DNA samples, taken her computer." He shrugged and shoveled some rice into his mouth. "If there's anything left for you to discover, it's going to be something that has no significance to law enforcement."

She held up a chopstick. "They don't know what we know, so what has no meaning for them might mean a great deal to us."

"This garlic chicken is making me thirsty." Sam pushed back from the table. "Can I get you something to drink?"

"Just water."

When he brought two glasses of water back to the table, she took a few gulps and shoved her plate away. "I'm done. I meant to change clothes when I got home. I'm not going to go digging around in the desert in a skirt."

"You had about two bites."

"No appetite." She crossed her chopsticks on the edge of her plate.

"You change and I'll finish eating. Then I'll feed Chip." Sam held up two fingers. "No garlic chicken for him, I swear."

"You'd better not. Dogs aren't supposed to have garlic." She placed a fork in front of him. "Use this, please, or we'll be here all night as you chase that chicken around your plate."

"I *am* getting kind of hungry." He grabbed the fork and plowed into the food.

She waved her hand over the table. "You're feeding Chip, so I'll clean up. Leave all this for me."

She spun around and headed toward the bedroom, averting her gaze from the bed. She couldn't look at it without a hot blush rushing to her cheeks. She'd been so darned easy after all her resolutions, but just because she'd taken Sam back into her bed, didn't mean she was letting him back into her heart—he had to earn his way back there.

She changed into the same outfit she'd worn to dump those bones—dark jeans, dark T-shirt and boots. She wanted to blend in with the night, just in case.

After she brushed her teeth and pulled her hair into a ponytail, she went back into the living room. "Did Chip eat?"

"Every morsel. I let him out back." Sam flicked a dish towel over his shoulder. "Cleaned up, too."

"You didn't have to do that."

"You know these newfangled inventions like a dishwasher and refrigerator make it easy. I just stuck the cartons into the fridge and put the dishes in the dishwasher." He narrowed his eyes. "You look ready for a covert operation."

"Isn't that what this is? We're taking this seriously, aren't we?" She shoved her hands in her back pockets and dug the heels of her boots into the floor. "You're not doing this to humor me, are you?"

"Humor you? It's gone beyond that with Melody's death." He flipped up his shirt to expose the gun at his waist. "Does this look like I'm not taking it seriously?"

She swallowed. "All right, then. Let's go."

Sam went to the sliding doors and whistled for Chip. "Is his dog door closed?"

"I keep it closed at night once he's inside." She raised her eyebrows. "Afraid I'll get more warnings left on my porch?"

"If all you got were a few dead snakes with arrows through their heads, I'd be happy. Just keep your house locked up and Chip on guard."

Jolene grabbed a backpack with a flashlight, a spade, a bottle of water and some other essential items for creeping through the night in the desert.

She tripped to a stop on the porch when she saw Sam's Border Patrol truck parked behind the rental car that had been delivered to her today in the driveway. "You're on Border Patrol business?"

"Our agency isn't as particular about company vehicles as yours is. Did you think I was going to take that little rental into the sand? We'd get stuck in two minutes." He strode to the truck and opened the back. "Throw your stuff in here, and open your garage door so we can take a few tools."

"Tools?" She entered the code for her garage door.

"Don't tell me you dug through the sand to

bury those bones with your two hands. I know you have a shovel. I saw it, remember?"

She ducked under the garage door before it finished opening and grabbed the shovel she'd used earlier in the week. "Anything else?"

"That's good enough." He took the shovel from her and threw it in the back of the truck.

As she climbed into the truck, the wind picked up and snatched at her ponytail. She tipped her head back and sniffed the air. "I hope there's not another monsoon on the way."

"Wouldn't surprise me." Sam slammed her door and went around to the driver's side. He started the truck and rolled down her driveway.

They rode in silence for a few miles with the radio playing in the background. Jolene gazed out the window and took a deep breath. "You never showed me any pictures of Jess."

"You never asked."

"D-do you have some on your phone?" She folded her hands in her lap. "I'd like to see them… her."

"I do." He snatched up his phone on the console and entered his passcode with his thumb. He dropped the phone in her lap. "If you go to my photos, you'll see a whole folder dedicated to her."

With unsteady hands, Jolene picked up his phone and accessed the folder called *Jess*. In the first picture, a bright-eyed toddler with curly dark hair grinned back at her.

Jolene's own lips stretched into a smile almost involuntarily. "She looks like you…and she looks full of mischief."

"She is." Sam's chest almost puffed up. "She's still small for her age, but her pediatrician says she'll catch up. She likes books. She likes anything with wheels, and she loves dogs. I showed her a picture of Chip when he was a puppy, and now she calls every dog Chip."

Tears pricked the back of Jolene's eyes, and the next picture of Jess riding a plastic Big Wheel blurred before her. "Sounds like you'll have to get her a dog."

"I will when she's older. I…" Sam stopped and his hands tightened on the steering wheel. "She's funny. She makes me laugh."

Jolene swiped through several more photos of the happy little girl. She'd made the right choice letting Sam go. Would he have been able to have the same kind of relationship with his daughter living apart from her? Living in another state? And with Aimee using again, he'd have never known a moment's peace.

She let out a sigh and placed his phone back on the console. "She's adorable."

"I want you to meet her, Jolene."

Tapping on the window, she said, "It's coming up. We can take the access road to the casino construction site, and then I'll guide you in from there."

Sam slowed the truck, but they didn't have to search for the entrance to the access road this time. A huge orange-and-yellow sign had gone up on the road, proclaiming this the future site of the Yaqui Desert Sun Casino.

The sign made her stomach churn. Her father had died here and it meant nothing to the people he'd led and counseled most of his life. She licked her lips. "Cheerful sign, huh?"

Sam glanced at her. "If you like that sort of thing."

As he pulled onto the access road, sand pinged the windshield of the truck. "It's windy out here tonight. If it brings in a storm, we're gonna abandon ship and do this another night."

"Yeah, well, I'm sure we're going to have a limited number of nights before the bones are dismissed as a stunt." She sat forward in her seat. "The equipment is still here. The builders must think they'll be back to work soon."

"Maybe they will." The truck crawled to a stop, idling at the edge of the construction site, the out-of-commission equipment hulking in the darkness like the bones of some extinct creatures. "Where to?"

She closed her eyes and mumbled a few words, tracing lines in the air with her fingertip.

"What are you doing? Is that an old Yaqui spell?"

She punched his arm. "Remember the map that was stolen?"

"Of course—the map you didn't accuse Wade of stealing because you didn't want him to know you had stolen the map from him in case he didn't realize you'd stolen the map. That map?"

"Yes." She tapped her head. "I memorized it—or at least the construction areas. There were other sections shaded in blue that were not yet earmarked for building. I think we should start there."

Sam peered over the steering wheel out the window. "You're going to know where to go from here without a compass, exact measurements and surveying equipment? We don't even have light."

"I have something better. The land has already been divided and marked. This open plot is all for show, for the ground-breaking, to make it look like this is the first time the developers are dipping into the land. Of course, it's not." She smacked the dashboard. "Drive forward. We'll see posts with markings on them that indicate the different areas of the casino. The buffet restaurant is at the south end of the complex and beyond that? Wasteland."

"I do have a compass in this truck, and we'll

head south." He put the truck into gear and cranked the wheel to the left.

The truck went off the road, dipping and tipping along the desert floor. Neither Sam's nor her rental would've been able to navigate this terrain.

She grabbed his forearm. "Stop. You see that post up ahead with the reflective lights?"

"Uh-huh. One of the markers?"

"Yeah. I'll jump out and see what it says." She reached into the back seat of the truck and yanked her backpack into her lap. She dug into the main compartment and pulled out her flashlight. "I'll be right back."

She launched from the truck and rushed to the post. The less time she spent out here with the snakes and scorpions, the better—and she didn't mean the reptile and bug kind. Those she could handle.

She aimed her flashlight at the post, the beam picking out the letters. Then she scurried back to the truck and hopped in, panting just a little. "That's the lobby and customer service area. As I recall from the map, we can keep following this outer edge to the buffet. Do you see the temporary fence along here?"

"Yeah, I'll try not to veer into it and take it out."

As the truck trundled along what would be the west side of the casino complex, Jolene sat forward in her seat, taking note of each signpost. Their cessation would signal the end of the planned structure.

Sam whistled. "This is going to be a big place."

"Is that a post up ahead?" She squinted into the area flooded by the truck's brights. "It looks shorter and thicker. Don't hit it."

"I'm not going to hit it." He crept up to the post and threw the truck into Park. "Check it out."

Once more, she slid from the truck, the wind whipping her hair as she approached and lit up the four squat posts. Her fingers traced over the letters, her heart thumping.

When she got back in the truck, she turned to face Sam. "This is it. Those posts indicate the end of the dining area and the end of the building."

Sam tipped his head. "Then it's no-man's-land ahead."

"Yep."

"We're close to the border. I guess that makes it easier for the Yaqui in Mexico to come across and work in the casino."

"That's the idea." Jolene squashed down the niggling guilt she felt about the excitement the Yaqui on the other side of the border had about the coming project and their part in it.

"Yaqui land stretches right to the border and beyond, doesn't it?"

"That's why we need to be careful in your Bor-

der Patrol truck, Sam. Border Patrol has no juris-
diction at this border."

"Don't I know it. The map detailing the tunnels the cartel Las Moscas constructed along the
border stopped short of Yaqui land."

She rapped on the window. "This is definitely
the shaded area on the map—the no-go zone for
construction."

"I wonder why." Sam drummed his thumbs
on the steering wheel. "I think this is where we
need to investigate."

As she grabbed the door handle of the truck,
Sam put his hand on her arm. "Is this the area
where your father's body was discovered?"

She nodded and pushed open the door.

The wind gusted, and she shielded her eyes
against the grains of sand zinging through the
air. Sam had left his headlights on, creating a
lighted area.

With her head down, Jolene plowed through
the sand toward the spot flooded with light. She
studied the ground for anything unusual, any disruption to the plants or the rocks scattered about.

Sam had joined her, flicking his flashlight
along the edge of the lighted region. "They
haven't done anything to this section yet."

Scuffing along the ground, Jolene said, "You'd
think they'd want to utilize the entire property,

but I think they do plan on making a resort out of the place and this land figured into that."

Sam jerked his head up. "Did you hear that noise?"

Jolene held her breath, cocking her head to one side. When the wind blasted, she could hear a whooshing sound and the sand pinging Sam's truck, and when the wind died back down, the plaintive hoot of an owl echoed across the landscape.

"Nothing. What did you hear?"

"Thought I heard a buzzing sound." He kicked at a rock. "At least there's not much trash out here from the highway. Maybe the builders pick it up after a stiff breeze like tonight—just to keep on everyone's good side."

"They're not on my good side." Hands on her hips, Jolene scanned the ground, bit by bit, to the edge of the lighted area.

"I don't see anything, do you?" Sam had already turned back toward the truck.

"Nothing that would scream graveyard, anyway." She followed in his very large footsteps. "Keep going?"

"I want to continue to the border. See if it's more of the same."

When they both got into the truck, Sam put it into gear and eased it forward. "We don't need to get stuck out here. That would be a lot for me to explain."

The truck rumbled ahead, and Sam made a

beeline for the border only he saw in his head. "It should be along here in less than a mile. They're gonna have to make some accommodations for the people coming over from Mexico to work in the casino."

They bounced along for a few more minutes before Sam slowed down and stopped. "Let's take a look."

As they stood outside the truck, Jolene asked, "Do you know where the border is?"

"It's beyond that ridge. When the land officials drew these borders, they didn't necessarily follow any geographic patterns—unless they could."

Sam raised a pair of binoculars to his eyes, more interested in the land beyond than the land below their feet.

Jolene aimed her flashlight at the ground, skimming it along the foliage. Every time the wind kicked up, flurries of sand danced in circles and bits of debris rolled along the desert floor.

Her light caught a piece of plastic or something that a Saguaro cactus had caught, and she crept toward it to peel it from the plant's spines.

As she reached for it, a loud report buffeted her ears, followed by something whizzing past her head.

Sam shouted, "Get down. Someone's shooting at us."

Chapter Thirteen

Sam hit the ground and twisted around to locate Jolene, hunched down by a large cactus. He yelled at her as another gunshot blasted from the ridge, along with a flash of light. "Down! Flat on the ground. Get behind that cactus, if you can."

He army-crawled toward her, shifting the binoculars onto his back and reaching for the weapon on his hip. Sand needled his eyes and slipped into his mouth as he made his way to Jolene.

Glass exploded as a bullet hit one of the truck's headlights. Sam dug in faster to reach Jolene, half of her body behind the saguaro and her legs jutting out, exposed.

He wrapped a hand around her ankle and she squealed.

"It's me. We're gonna crawl back to the truck. Stay as low as you can, burrow into the sand as much as possible. The shooters aren't too bright. They already knocked out one of the headlights, giving them less visibility."

He finally got his gun free, and he twisted his body, raised the weapon and shot out the other headlight. "There. They're gonna have an even harder time taking aim at us."

Placing himself between Jolene and the ridge, which was the source of the shooting, Sam crawled, using one elbow to propel himself while clutching his gun in the other hand.

They didn't stop moving and Sam didn't stop panting until they reached the truck. He'd left the doors open, so he half shoved, half lifted Jolene into the passenger seat. "Keep your head down. Are you okay?"

"I'm fine, terrified, but unharmed."

"Don't shut your door until I'm in the truck. I don't want to give them any sound to follow until I can gun this vehicle." He slinked back to the ground and crawled underneath the truck to get to the other side.

The shooting had stopped, but he didn't trust that the gunmen weren't on their way to the truck right now to continue their assault.

As he pulled himself up, the buzzing sound he'd heard before grew louder, and Jolene yelped.

"It's…it's… There's a drone, Sam. A drone is hovering above the truck."

"Damn." The drone glinted for a second, and then dipped out of view.

Sam hunched behind the wheel and said, "Shut your door now."

They both slammed their doors at the same time and Sam cranked on the engine. As much as he wanted to floor it and get the hell out of there, he didn't want to get stuck. He threw the gear into Reverse and eased on the gas pedal.

Even though he still had his head down, he didn't have to worry about hitting anything out here…except maybe a cactus. The truck rolled back, and he applied more pressure to the accelerator. The wheels ran over something, and then he shifted into Drive and took off in the direction of the construction area and the access road.

Several seconds later, his head popped up and the dark landscape loomed in front of him. "I can't see much without the headlights."

Jolene answered in a muffled voice, "Can I come up for air now?"

"I think we're okay." He glanced in his rearview mirror and didn't see anything coming—no light, no more gunfire. "We're good."

She straightened up, clutching her flashlight. "Do you have your flashlight? I can use both of them to shed a little light on our exit route."

"It's in my backpack, which I forgot is still on my back." He leaned forward. "Can you get it?"

She tugged at the pack, and he released the

steering wheel so she could pull it from his arms. She dug into it and retrieved his flashlight.

"Let me try this." She rolled down her window and aimed both flashlights at the ground in front of the truck. "Does that help?"

"At least I won't go plowing into a cactus. Are we almost out of no-man's-land? We can follow the reflective posts back to the access road."

"Shouldn't be too much farther." She reached out and tapped the side mirror with one of the flashlights. "Do you think they'll come after us?"

"Doubt it. They know I'm armed, at any rate. Maybe that'll be enough to keep them away unless they want to engage in a gun battle."

"I should've brought Dad's gun with me."

"We don't need any more bullets flying." He jerked the steering wheel to the side. "Is that the edge of the casino?"

"Yeah, you've got this."

Tense silence loomed in the truck as Sam navigated his way out of the construction area and back onto the access road. He glanced at Jolene's ramrod-straight spine as she held the flashlights to help him navigate the terrain.

They both let out sighs when the truck tires gained purchase on the dirt road that would take them out to the highway. Once on the asphalt, Sam floored it and the truck lurched forward, eating up the road beneath them.

"Do you still need the flashlights?"

"I'm good. I know this section of the highway like the back of my hand." He punched on the emergency lights. "Just for some extra visibility, although I don't think we'll meet many cars at this time of night."

"I hope we don't meet anyone." She flicked off the flashlights and collapsed against the seat, rubbing the back of her neck.

"Is your neck still bothering you?"

"I think it's just from holding my muscles so tight." She wound her ponytail around her hand. "What happened back there—I mean besides the obvious?"

"Someone's patrolling that area with a drone and I'm guessing that drone has a camera attached to it."

"It's not you guys?" She sucked in her bottom lip.

"We have drones on the border, but Yaqui land is off-limits to us." He nudged her shoulder. "You know that. Your father was one of the most vocal voices against our patrolling that section of the border, partly because he didn't feel the Yaqui needed any division between the Mexican tribe and the American tribe."

"Yeah, that was Dad. He had an almost childlike faith in humanity—never mind that the

Yaqui across the border weren't all that interested in mingling with us."

"They are now." Sam swiped a bead of sweat
from his forehead. "Maybe Wade accomplished
with the casino what your father couldn't accom-
plish without it."

"You're probably right." She wedged her hands
between her knees. "So, someone—not the Border Patrol—has drones on the border. Do you
think it's the builders? And do you think they
caught us on camera?"

"It might be the developers, but if they have
armed guys shooting at trespassers instead of
calling the Sheriff's Department, they're not
going to want to admit they're the ones monitoring the drone footage."

"So, you think that's how they knew we were
there? They were checking the video from the
drone and saw us?" She brushed dust and sand
from her jeans, and it settled in a fine layer on
the truck mat. Stirring it with the toe of her boot,
she said, "Sorry."

"Yeah, I think I have bigger problems with
this truck than a little sand on the floor." Sam
beeped the horn at a car coming at them in the
other lane. The car honked back and flicked his
lights on and off. "If the developers are the ones
with the drones, their guys overreacted."

"Unless they weren't shooting to kill. Maybe they were just shooting to scare us off."

"Every time you have a gun in your hand, there's a chance someone's going to end up dead, so that's a stupid plan if that's the case." He wiped the back of his hand across his mouth, but he'd need to rinse with some water if he hoped to get the sand out of his teeth. "Or these shooters are not connected to the developer—and they're watching that land for another reason."

"You mean like there's something buried there they don't want anyone to find?"

"Maybe." Sam screwed up his mouth and chewed on the inside of his cheek. "There was something about that terrain."

Jolene slapped his arm. "Don't do that with your mouth. It's a bad habit."

"One of many." He banged his fist on the horn again as another car approached. "I'm going to have to take the back way into town to avoid rolling down Main Street with two busted headlights on my Border Patrol truck."

"What are you going to tell them?"

"A half-truth." He lifted one shoulder. He hated admitting to Jolene that he planned to tell a lie, even half of a lie. "I'll tell them someone shot out the headlights, but I won't tell them the circumstances. Because once I tell them the circumstances, my interest in that property is going to be common knowledge."

"Don't tell them…if you can get away with it, and you won't get into any trouble."

"Lies always cause trouble, don't they?" He ran a hand down the thigh of her dirty jeans. "Scared the hell out me when I realized someone was taking potshots at us. All I could think of was that I couldn't lose you after I'd…we'd, after I'd seen you again."

He snuck a peek at her profile, stony and mute, her lips pressed together.

He blew out a breath. "Anyway, I'm glad you weren't hurt."

"Me, too. I mean, I'm glad you weren't hurt."

He'd take that. He swallowed, the grains of sand scratching his throat.

When he finally turned onto Jolene's street, his shoulders dropped and he tried to roll out the tightness. They could've been killed out there.

He parked the truck behind her rental, and they dragged their stuff out, shaking the sand off in her driveway. The wind had settled, but a fat raindrop hit the back of his hand.

"Looks like the wind brought in another storm."

Jolene folded her arms across her zipped-up hoodie and tilted her head back. "It's a good thing we got here before the rain started. Driving with no headlights was bad enough but doing it on slick roads would've made it ten times worse."

He followed her to the garage door, and she opened it using the keypad on the side. As it creaked open, Sam ducked under and returned her shovel to the corner.

Jolene jingled her keys as she walked up to the door that connected the garage to the house, Chip scratching and whining all the way. She unlocked the door and pressed her thumb against the control to close the garage.

"God, what a night." Sam tossed his backpack onto the floor. "All that shooting made me crave Chinese. Do you want some leftovers?"

"Yeah, but I refuse to eat it cold, like you usually do." She drew up close to him, practically touching her nose to his and his pulse jumped. She dabbed at his cheek with her fingertip. "You have a little dried blood there. Did the glass hit you?"

"Probably." He scraped at the spot and winced at the stinging sensation.

"You just made it bleed." She yanked a piece of paper towel from the holder and ran some water over it.

Closing his eyes, he held still as she pressed it gently against his face. He wanted to take her in his arms right now and lose himself in her kisses.

Revel in her warm body when he could've lost her out there.

She took his hand and replaced her fingers with his on the paper towel. "Hold it there for a few seconds. It'll stop bleeding. It's just a little ding on that otherwise perfect face."

His eyelids flew open. Was that a come-on?

"Ugh, I have sand everywhere from crawling on the ground." She grabbed the zipper on her hoodie and yanked it down. The hoodie crackled as she peeled it from her body. She hung it over the back of a chair as she smacked some kind of plastic wrapper on the kitchen table.

Sam raised his eyebrows. "What is that?"

"It blew across the ground and got stuck on that cactus. I grabbed it right before the shooting started and stuffed it inside my sweatshirt. I don't know why. It was just the biggest piece of trash out there."

"Let me see that." He tossed the wet paper towel sporting his blood into the trash, and smoothed his hand across the heavy plastic. "There's a label on this."

Jolene sidled up next to him and peered over his shoulder. "What's it say?"

Sam swiped away some of the dirt, careful not to smear the letters, which were neatly typed out like a label printed from a computer. The black lettering jumped out at him, and a spike of adrenaline jacked him up.

Jolene ran a finger beneath the words. "There's a date, and the words say… *Pink Lady.* There's a drink called Pink Lady. What is this, packaging for some booze?"

She flicked the edge of the plastic wrapping and turned away.

"Jolene, this is the type of label the cartels use to wrap and ID their product."

"What?" She spun around, knocking into a chair.

"Pink Lady is the meth I was telling you about, the meth that's connected to those dead bodies. Do you know what this means?" He grabbed the plastic and shook it.

She nodded once. "The cartels are using Yaqui land to smuggle drugs."

Chapter Fourteen

Jolene sank to the chair. "Maybe the Pima County Sheriffs were right all along. Maybe my dad's murder *was* related to the cartels, but he did more than stumble across a few mules, didn't he?"

"This connects a lot of dots." Sam slammed the packaging back on the table and paced to the corner of the room and back, Chip trotting at his heels. "You know how I was looking at that ridge and the landscape with my binoculars before the gunfire?"

"You mentioned you noticed something about the land out there, but never finished the thought."

"We got our hands on a map of tunnels the Las Moscas cartel was using to smuggle drugs into this country. The agents in this region have been going out to each tunnel to close it and destroy it. I had the chance to study all of the tunnels, and they shared some common features."

"A ridge, some brush."

After watching Sam's back-and-forth, Jolene

pushed back her chair and grabbed Chip's collar. "Get on your bed, Chip."

The dog gave Sam one hopeful look before slinking to his bed in the corner, fluffing it up with his paws and plopping into it.

"Good boy." Jolene gripped the back of a kitchen chair. "Pink Lady? Didn't you tell me the pure form of meth that accompanied the disappearances in San Diego was pink in color?"

"Yeah, that's it. On the street, they call it Pinky."

"Pinky?" Jolene dug her nails into the chair. "That's what Tucker called Melody."

"Sad coincidence." Sam tripped to a stop. "Melody hadn't added drugs to her other bad habits, had she?"

"Not that I know of, but what *do* I know?" She picked up the chair and settled it closer to the table. "I had no idea she was drinking again. I was a terrible cousin and friend, and on the very night she died, I was romping it up in bed—with you."

"Great, now you're adding guilt to the myriad reasons why you shouldn't have slept with me."

Jolene clenched her jaw to keep it from dropping open. Was that what he thought? That she regretted hooking up with him? Didn't she?

Casting her eyes down, she said, "Doesn't it feel wrong now?"

"Being with you would never feel wrong to me. Look at it this way." He folded his arms and wedged a shoulder against the sliding door. "Melody introduced us. She wanted us to get back together. Maybe she was leading us to each other."

She blinked. Sam had a fanciful side? "One thing I am going to do is try to make sense of her death, and I'm going to start by searching her apartment tomorrow."

"Then you'd better get to sleep tonight. I'm going to figure out a way to search for a tunnel on that property."

"Wade would never allow that." She ran her hand over the plastic packaging. "You think the cartels have a tunnel from Yaqui land on the Mexican side of the border to our land, and they're smuggling drugs…or *were* smuggling drugs through this tunnel?"

"I do think that. The group that's manufacturing this pink meth and putting it on the street requires such anonymity they're willing to kill off their mules to make sure they keep secrets."

"That's what happened in San Diego?"

"All the bodies we found and identified matched up to suspected mules. Someone met them when they made it across the border, and then murdered them to keep them quiet."

"Why do that? Cartels have used mules for

ages. Sometimes they do go rogue, but the cartels have always been able to deal with those people."

Sam tugged on his earlobe. "This particular group...or person wants to lay low. I wonder if Melody knew El Gringo Viejo was behind Pink Lady. That would explain a lot. He wouldn't want the cartels to know he was infringing on their business."

"How would she know that, Sam? Melody didn't hang out with that crowd." She put two fingers on her lips.

"What? Did you remember something?"

"That relationship she had, the one Wade broke up. The guy was bad news. I think he may have been involved with the drug trade. Maybe she learned something from him."

"Do you remember his name?"

"Gabe, Gabe Altamarino. I think he's in Tucson, now."

"I think we need to pay him a visit and tell him the sad news about Melody."

"And the casino? What does this all have to do with the casino?"

"I'm not sure yet. It has to do with the land, doesn't it? Maybe the cartel is holding something over the investors." Sam rubbed his eyes. "I'm done. I don't even want the Chinese food anymore. I just want a soft bed and sleep."

"About that..." Jolene wrinkled up her nose

"…I need more time to think about that, about us. I'm sorry if I led you on last night."

Sam bent over and scratched Chip behind the ear. "Don't worry about it. It's all good, no expectations. Can I have the spare room, or should I leave?"

She'd hurt him, disappointed him. "Of course, you can stay here. I'm not going to kick you out to your truck with no headlights, especially since you saved my life tonight."

"I couldn't have gotten that truck out of there without you." He held up his hands. "And I promise I won't even use your washer and dryer this time."

"Have you seen the spare room? I turned it into a combination office and gym. There's no bed in there anymore."

He eyed the couch with Chip now curled up on one end. "The sofa's fine. Not much left of this night, anyway."

"You don't have to sleep out here…with Chip." She walked into the kitchen to hide her warm face. "I mean, you can share my bed, if…you know."

Inviting a man like Sam Cross into her bed with no promise of sex was like expecting a dog not to scratch his fleas. Bad analogy.

"You are irresistible, Jolene, but I think I can manage to keep my hands…and everything else…to myself in your presence."

Her cheeks flamed as she spun around. "I didn't mean it like that."

A grin spread across his handsome face. "I'm teasing you. I'd much rather share a bed with you than Chip, so I'm accepting your offer, strings and all, but I'm gonna need a shower first. I have sand in places that, well, you're never gonna discover tonight."

"I do, too. I'm like that cartoon character with a permanent cloud of dirt over my head."

"You first. I have a few things to check on my phone."

"Deal." She escaped the uncomfortable conversation and hightailed it to the bedroom.

She stripped off her clothes in the bathroom, leaving a pile of sand on the tile floor. Keeping her hair in a ponytail, she soaped up and rinsed off, showering in record time.

She pulled on a pair of pajamas—tops and bottoms—and slipped between the sheets.

Sam tapped on the door. "Everyone decent?"

"C'mon in."

He pushed open the door. "Everything's locked up. I let Chip out once more, and I started the dishwasher."

"Thanks, Sam. The bathroom's all yours." She yawned in an exaggerated manner. "I'm going to fall asleep in about two minutes."

"I'll keep it down." He moved silently across

the room to the bathroom and clicked the door closed.

Her ears tuned in to every rustle and scrape from the other room. When the water started, she squeezed her eyes closed, visions of water sluicing over Sam's hard body making her mouth water.

She didn't have to worry about Sam controlling himself. She had to watch herself. When had she ever been able to resist that man? Only at the end, when she knew he had to be there for his baby.

The water stopped, and she clenched her muscles, holding herself still. By the time he exited the bathroom on a rush of citrus-scented steam, she was wide-awake.

He flipped back one corner of the covers and crawled into bed behind her, his warm, slightly damp skin giving off some kind of magnetic wave to pull her in.

She held her breath as he settled in, managing to avoid all contact with her body. Then she cursed herself for holding her breath because she had to let it out.

She puckered her lips and blew it out. It sounded like a gale-force wind, but Sam didn't move a muscle. As she lay there listening to his breathing, it deepened. Sam didn't snore a lot or loudly, but a few snuffles and snorts indicated that he was off to dreamland. Wish she could say the same.

About an eternity later, Sam shifted and his knee wedged just beneath her bottom. When he didn't move it, she knew he'd reached nirvana—sound asleep while she still tossed and turned, or at least tossed and turned in her mind because she was in the exact same spot she had been in when Sam joined her in bed.

They should've just made love—she'd be asleep by now—asleep and satisfied and no more confused that she was now.

JOLENE JERKED AWAKE the next morning and scrambled out of bed. Sam had gotten up before her again. He'd obviously gotten more sleep than she had.

His voice, sounding way too cheerful for morning, greeted her from the kitchen. "I found some pancake mix. You want some pancakes?"

She tossed her grungy ponytail over her shoulder. "You've turned into a regular Suzy Homemaker. I don't remember you cooking one thing when...we were together."

"I told you, Jess changed everything. Full disclosure—" he held up a spatula "—I do have a housekeeper who comes in once a week, and I drop Jess off at day care when I'm working."

"Is it hard?" She tipped her head. "Is it hard

being a single dad? Because that's what you are. How much time does Jess spend with Aimee?"

"As little as I can possibly get away with." His lips twisted and he flipped a pancake. "I made coffee, too."

She lifted her nose and sniffed. "I smell it."

"Sit down and eat." He held out a plate stacked with pancakes. "Do you have syrup in the fridge?"

"I think so." She took the plate with one hand and a coffee mug with the other. "Chip?"

"Fed him."

Hearing his name, Chip thumped his tail twice, obviously too sated to even get up and greet her.

"You're spoiling that dog." Jolene pulled out a chair. "How'd you sleep?"

"Great. I was beat." He pulled out the chair across from her and sat down with his own plate. "You?"

"I slept really well, too." She could lie with the best of them. "Do you need to go into the station today? My boss heard about Melody and told me to take another few days off, and I figured we… I could go to Melody's place this morning."

"I can join you. I have to bring the truck back and make some excuses for its condition. I also want to pick up that map of Las Moscas tunnels." Sam squeezed a puddle of syrup onto his pancakes.

"But that map didn't show a tunnel on Yaqui land, right?"

"I'm sure the tunnel I suspect is on Yaqui land is not one of Las Moscas'—or it *would* have been on that map. It's someone else. Someone who wants to maintain a covert presence, someone who doesn't want to upset the cartels. In short, El Gringo."

Jolene stirred some milk into her coffee. "The appearance of Pink Lady must've upset the cartels if it was that pure. It must've demanded a high price, higher than the regular meth coming across."

"Oh, it did, but it showed up in small quantities. It wasn't replacing the lower grade stuff by a long shot."

"Is it still on the street in San Diego?"

"It is." He cleared his throat before sawing into his pancakes. "They got to the mules *after* they crossed the border. The product had been taken off them before they were killed."

"That's so brutal." She shivered and took a sip of the hot coffee. "It's like he wants to wipe out everyone who knows about the origins of Pink Lady, but that can't be Melody."

"Maybe Melody didn't know about the origins of Pink Lady, but she had an idea of how it was connected to the casino and she'd heard about El Gringo Viejo." Sam stuffed the last of his pancakes in his mouth. "I'm going to head out to the station now and then go back to my motel to shower and change. I'll pick you up later, and we'll try to get into Melody's place."

As Jolene watched Sam back his truck out of her driveway, it felt like someone had punched her in the gut. No affection from him this morning, no kiss, no double entendre about sharing a bed—no nothing.

Had she just made the biggest mistake of her life?

An hour later, she blew out a sigh of relief when she saw Sam's rental car pull up in front of her house. Not that she doubted he'd return—he *did* want to get into Melody's place—but the last time she'd rejected him, he'd taken her at her word.

She patted Chip's head and said, "I get him all to myself this time, buddy."

She stepped out onto the porch and waved before Sam had a chance to leave his car. When she dipped inside the car, she said, "How'd it go with the truck?"

"I didn't have to answer too many questions—about that."

She shot him a glance from the corner of her eye. "What then?"

"If I'd found anything yet to justify my presence in Paradiso. I was appropriately vague." He patted his bag in the back seat. "And I got a copy of the tunnel map, courtesy of Nash Dillon." He lifted an eyebrow. "Nash invited me to the big bash in Tucson tomorrow night celebrating the casino. I'm sure you were invited. Why didn't you tell me?"

"I wasn't planning on going, and I wasn't sure they were still having it. They must be confident those bones I buried there aren't some long-lost Yaqui."

"They must be." He started the car and pulled away from her house. "Anyway, we're going."

"We are?"

"It might be an opportunity to find out more about the investors in the casino."

Jolene covered her mouth. "I almost forgot Nash's consortium has an investment in the Desert Sun Casino. Do you think he knows anything about a connection to the cartels?"

"Nash?" Sam snorted. "If Nash thought there was anything fishy about that property, he'd pull out. Truth is, he has more to do with the pecan-processing business than the other investments. He and his family leave that up to the partners."

"The gala tomorrow is a fancy dress-up thing. You ready for that?" She eyed his broad shoulders. She'd never seen Sam dressed to the nines before—and she'd like to.

"I can rent a tux in Tucson. It might not be a perfect fit, but I'm sure I'll be presentable."

He'd be more than presentable. "Then it's a date."

"Are *you* ready for it? You didn't plan to go."

"I have a few things that'll work. I wonder if Wade is still going."

"I'm not saying Wade's a cold dude, but I don't think the death of his sister is going to keep him from this. He's been waiting too long."

"I think you're right." Jolene sucked in a breath. "The crime scene tape is still up. Is it off-limits?"

"They're done collecting evidence from her place. There are no cops watching it, and you know where Melody kept a spare key, if it's still there. I say, we go for it."

He parked the car at the edge of the parking lot in front of the building, just like he had the previous time. Then they'd been accosted by Tucker. Who knew what would happen this time?

Jolene strode across the parking lot, not looking left or right, putting on a casual, noncommittal face—the type of face you wouldn't wear when attempting to search your dead cousin's apartment.

She tripped on the first step, and Sam grabbed her arm. "Hold on. You're acting like you're on your way to a demolition. Slow down. Take a few deep breaths. You're here to find suitable clothing for Melody's burial—if anyone asks."

Nodding, she filled her lungs with air, realizing that she'd been holding her breath all the way across the parking lot. She continued up the stairs without a mishap, or maybe that was due to Sam's steadying hand on her back.

He was still here for her, even though she'd relegated him to a tiny, cold corner of her bed last night, although he seemed to have minded it less than she had.

When they reached Melody's door, Sam ran a finger along the crime scene tape and held it out while Jolene crouched beside the middle pot in a row of wilted plants. She dug the key from the dirt, blew it off and held it up to Sam. They both ducked under the yellow tape, and Jolene clicked the door shut behind them.

As she turned to face the room, her nose twitched. Melody hadn't been dead long when they'd discovered her body, but the room still smelled like death. She made a wide berth around the red stain on the tile floor next to the coffee table.

"Where do we start?"

"With these." Sam dug in his backpack and pulled out two pairs of gloves. "Just in case. We don't need any more of our prints around here."

Jolene waved at the little table in the corner of

the room, printer cables dangling over the edge like spiders' legs. "That's where she had her computer. So, I guess we can't check that."

"Drawers, shelves, pictures, closets. You might notice something that escaped the cops' attention." Sam snapped on his gloves. "I'll start in here. Why don't you hit the bedroom? One or two?"

"Just one bedroom, one bath." Crossing the room, Jolene tugged on the gloves. She stepped into Melody's bedroom, her gaze tracking across the unmade bed and the closet and drawers spilling their guts. "The police did a number in here."

Sam called back, "They're not paying a social call."

Jolene mumbled under her breath as she plucked the comforter from the floor. "They could be a little more respectful."

She yanked open a nightstand drawer and pulled out a dog-eared paperback. She tossed it on the bed, no better than the cops who'd trashed the place earlier. The book had been covering a box of condoms and some... Jolene picked up the silver bottle and squinted at the blue label—intimacy lotion. Jolene dropped the bottle. Good thing she was wearing these gloves.

Whatever Melody had been up to, she'd been getting more action than Jolene had.

As she shoved the drawer back into place, it

stuck. Jolene jiggled it, but the drawer wouldn't close.

She pulled it out as far as it would go, and then stuck her arm into the drawer, her fingers wiggling toward the back and through the space at the end.

The folded edge of a piece of paper met her touch. She couldn't fit her thumb into the gap, so she pinched the paper between the pad of her middle finger and the top of her index finger, the gloves giving her a little traction. She worked it loose and pulled it free.

"What are you doing in here? I called you three times." Sam appeared, framed in the doorway, grasping the doorjamb on either side with gloved hands.

"Trying to get this piece of paper wedged behind the drawer." She shook it out, and scanned a list of names, most of them crossed out. Melody's ex's name was on the list, conspicuously not crossed out. "Ugh, I hope I didn't just stumble on a list of Melody's conquests, although it must've been before she bagged Gabe because his name isn't marked off—and it looks like she was into girls, too. Maybe it's something else—AA members or something."

"Can I see that?" A crease forming between his eyebrows, Sam launched into the room and snatched the paper from Jolene's hand.

"No need to get grabby. I'm happy to show you the paper, Sam…"

"Shh." He flapped the notepaper at her. "Jolene, this is a list of mules."

Her heart skipped a few beats, and she pressed a hand against her chest. "Drug mules? What was Melody doing with this list? Her name's not on it, is it?"

"It might as well be." He flattened the paper on the bed and smoothed his hand across it. "These are the people whose bodies I'm looking for— this is the list of the dead."

Chapter Fifteen

Sam stared at the familiar list of names, as Jolene gasped and dragged a pillow into her lap.

"*Missing*. You said they were missing persons."

"They're dead, Jolene. We know they're dead." His mouth twisted.

"Gabe Altamarino is on your list? Melody's ex-boyfriend?"

"This list is slightly different from mine. She has names on here that aren't crossed off, and yet they're on my list. She has others, like Gabe that I don't have at all."

"What's she doing with these names, Sam? Melody was no drug mule." She dropped the paperback book into the drawer and slid it closed.

"She wasn't but Gabe was, and she definitely knew what was going on at the construction site." He backtracked to the bedroom door and picked up the item he'd dropped. "I made my own discovery. That's why I was calling you."

"An arrow?" Jolene's hands curled into fists.

"The same kind of arrow in the snake head Chip brought inside."

"Looks like Melody, not Wade, was trying to warn you away from interfering."

"But at the end, she texted me *El Gringo Viejo*. She must've had second thoughts, or was so wasted she wasn't thinking at all."

"Maybe once she knew I was helping you, she figured she'd drop his name." The feathers tickled his fingers as he ran his hand along the end of the arrow. "We need to find Gabe Altamarino."

"I always had a suspicion Melody never stopped seeing Gabe, despite Wade's best efforts." Jolene flicked her finger at the paper. "With his name on this list, do you think he's in hiding? How'd he get away if he was carrying Pink Lady across the border while the others disappeared? That was over two years ago, and he certainly wasn't in hiding when he was dating Melody."

"I don't know. Maybe he was one of the first, and the dealer wasn't being as thorough at that time." Sam lifted his shoulders. "Do you think Melody stole the map from you for the same reason? I'd feel better knowing she was the one skulking around your house."

"I would, too, but I doubt she was the one who fixed my brakes, so someone other than Melody wants me to back off…us, wants us to back off after what happened last night." Jolene carefully folded the sheet of paper. "I'm sticking this in my purse."

Sam had a strong urge to snatch the paper from her again and burn it. He didn't want Jolene to be in possession of any of this stuff. "Don't go waving that around. Put it in your safe."

"I can do that."

Sam nodded at a suitcase in the closet. "As long as we're here, you should probably go ahead and pack up some of Melody's clothes. Maybe pick out something for her burial and make good on that lie."

Jolene's dark eyes sparkled with unshed tears as she nodded. "Are you going to try to find Gabe? Like I said, I think he moved to Tucson after the breakup, or the pretend breakup."

"I'll use the resources back at the station. I can drop you off at Granny Viv's with Melody's suitcase, if you want to go there." He waved the arrow. "I'm going to toss this."

Ten minutes later, Sam took Melody's suitcase from Jolene and carried it down the stairs. He stashed it in the trunk of his car and they drove to the reservation.

He pulled up beside the Nighthawks' shiny Tesla and cut the engine. "I'll help you with the suitcase, but I'm not going inside—and if Wade's in there, it wouldn't be a good idea to spout off at him again."

She ran her fingertip along the seam of her lips. "I'm not saying a word to him about anything—not even Gabe, unless you want me to do some prying."

"No prying. The guy had a record, right? It should be easy to track him in the system and get a current address on him. If Tucker the trucker hadn't landed so conveniently in the laps of the police, they probably would've run down Gabe and questioned him, anyway."

"Yeah, I just can't shake off the guilt that we put Tucker in their sights."

"Tucker put himself there by taking Melody's purse."

"But not her phone."

"Phone's still missing." Sam popped the trunk and exited the vehicle. He hauled the suitcase from the back and wheeled it over the gravel to Granny Viv's front door. "Give my best and condolences to everyone and stay out of trouble."

"I'll do that." She placed her hand on his arm. "Pick me up later?"

"Sure, and if you get a ride back to your place before that, dinner?"

"I'll be sick of casseroles by that time." She jerked her thumb over her shoulder. "I'm sure the neighbors are delivering food to Gran and Wade's family."

"No casseroles, then. I'll be in touch." He spun

around, leaving her on the porch. He could've gone inside, but he didn't do well with emotions like that. He'd pay his respects to Melody in his own way by attending a meeting here in Paradiso—the same one where he met Melody, who then introduced him to Jolene.

He owed her that.

As he pulled into the station, a team was headed out in the trucks. He called out the window to Clay, who told him one of the drones had picked up some suspicious activity at one of the sealed-off tunnels.

Yeah, he could tell Clay a thing or two about suspicious activity.

The call made the station quiet, and Sam waved to just one other agent moored to his desk, his ear glued to the phone.

He dropped into the chair behind his temporary desk and logged in to the computer. First order of business was to pull up the map to the Las Moscas tunnels and see which one was closest to the Yaqui land.

With the map in front of him on the display, he studied the red dots indicating the closed tunnels. His finger hovered over the one that was farthest west and closest to the casino property. He zoomed in on it and brought it up in an aerial view to analyze the landscape. He'd seen similar formations along the Yaqui land—right before someone started taking shots at him and Jolene.

He drew some boundaries on the screen and printed out the highlighted section of the map.

He'd need the tribe's approval to go hunting for a tunnel along the border of its property—and that meant Wade's approval. Would Wade really want that stigma attached to his casino project?

He stood up, stretched and retrieved his sheet of paper from the printer. On the way back to his desk, he stopped by the vending machines and got a soda. He needed the caffeine.

Sleeping next to Jolene with the hands-off directive had been hell last night. Did she think he was made of stone? Hard, cold rock? He'd been rock hard, all right, but there'd been nothing cold about it.

She hadn't fooled him for a second. She hadn't been able to sleep, either. When Jolene slept, she threw arms and legs around, grabbing and bunching covers, crowding his space. Last night, she lay there like a log, not moving a muscle. It had to have taken great control on her part to pull that off.

The question remained, why'd she do it? Why'd she shut him down? She'd slipped up the night before. Desire had taken over her common sense, or maybe Melody's death had shaken her up so much she needed someone close. That didn't mean she wanted him back.

He snapped the tab on his can and chugged half the soda before taking his seat in front of the computer again.

This time he accessed the NCIC and entered *Gabe Altamarino*. He stared at the blinking cursor and the blank screen. Hunching forward, he entered *Gabriel Altamarino*. The system gave him no love—kinda like Jolene.

He took a few sips of his drink, cradling the bubbles with his tongue. Then he tried various spellings of *Altamarino*. Got a hit for Gabe Marino, but his picture and profile didn't match someone who'd be involved with Melody.

How'd that happen? One of the reasons Wade had been hell-bent against Melody's relationship with this guy was because he had a record. So, where was his record? Drug crimes as an adult could not be expunged. Maybe Gabe had been a juvenile when he'd committed these offenses.

Sam rubbed his eyes and dug into his email from his office in San Diego.

Jorge, the other agent in the office, approached his desk with a thick file. "Thought you might be interested in seeing this."

"What is it?" Sam pushed back from his desk and propped up his feet.

"It's the preliminary crime scene report from

the Melody Nighthawk murder. You're the one who found her, right? Nabbed her killer?"

Sam wouldn't bet on that second statement, but he nodded. "Yeah, I knew Melody. She was my friend's cousin."

Jorge plopped the file on Sam's desk next to his feet. "The sheriff's office sent it over earlier. Basic autopsy, no toxicology yet, prints and other trace evidence."

They'd missed the list of drug mules in her nightstand drawer.

"Thanks, man." Sam dropped his feet from the desk and wheeled his chair in, flipping over the cover of the file folder.

He ran his finger down the first page of details, and then began shuffling through the pages. He stopped at the one listing the number of fingerprints found in Melody's apartment—looked like a list from Grand Central Terminal.

His prints were identified, as well as Jolene's, Wade's, Tucker's, a bunch of unknowns and several sets ID'd but not familiar to him—probably Melody's friends. The police had probably zeroed in on Tucker's prints being in the apartment and called it a day.

He glanced through the preliminary autopsy report. Time of death had already been nailed down, but a cause of death hadn't been determined yet. The medical examiner would want to look at the toxicology report before making anything official.

The rest of the pages slipped through his fingers as he thumbed through them until he got to the autopsy photos. He spread a few of them out on the desk and studied Melody's head wound. Must've been more than the blood loss that killed her.

The medical examiner had taken photos of the tattoos on Melody's body. Sam's throat got tight when he made out one on Melody's thigh that said *survivor.* Damn, he should've intervened when he saw her drunk.

He peeled up another photo from his desk of a tattoo across Melody's lower back. Squinting, he read out loud, "Chris."

Who the hell was Chris? Was that Melody's sponsor's name? Family member? Sam ticked off Jolene's family members on his fingers but didn't recall a Chris. One of her friends?

Friends. He shuffled back through to the beginning of the file, and pulled out the list of fingerprints in the apartment. Hadn't he seen a Chris on this sheet?

His gaze tracked down the page and stumbled over one name—Christopher Contreras. How had this guy been in Melody's apartment enough to leave several prints and merit ink on her body without anyone knowing about him? Jolene had never mentioned a Chris to him.

If the police had ID'd Contreras's prints, he had to be in the system, and Sam would bet good money the guy wasn't in there for being a teacher or public servant.

The keys on his computer clacked as he accessed the NCIC system again. He entered Contreras's name and got a hit. He brought up the guy's information, his blood humming as he read through Contreras's priors and his current address in Tucson.

He stabbed the key to send the file to the printer and picked up the phone.

Jolene answered breathlessly on the third ring. "Sam?"

"Are you ready? We're going to pay a visit to Gabe Altamarino, aka Chris Contreras."

Chapter Sixteen

Jolene stepped onto the porch of her grandmother's house, fanning herself. It almost felt cool out here compared to the heat generated by the family inside.

As Sam's car rolled in front of Gran's driveway, Jolene launched off the porch, a thousand questions bubbling at her lips. She grabbed at the car door before Sam even put the car in Park.

He popped the locks and she swooped inside, pulling the seat belt in after her to save time. "Who the heck is Christopher Contreras?"

"Chris Contreras is Gabe Altamarino."

"How do you know that?" She snapped on her seat belt and rapped on the dashboard. "Go, go."

Sam plucked up a folded sheet of paper nestled on the console between them and shook it out. "Is this Gabe?"

Dark eyes pinned her in their gaze from the thin face of a man with a goatee and wavy hair swept back from a high forehead. "It's Gabe."

"That's what I thought." He dropped the sheet of paper where it floated to her lap. "His real name is Chris Contreras."

"Is that name in the criminal database you use?" She folded the paper to escape those eyes. She hadn't much cared for Gabe in person and didn't like him any better in one dimension.

"No. That was the problem. I entered *Gabe Altamarino* in the system and no criminal record was returned. I then…uh, looked at Melody's autopsy photos." He squeezed her fingers. "Sorry."

Jolene swallowed. "What did they tell you?"

"Melody had a tattoo on her lower back with the name Chris. Did you know that?"

"Haven't hung out at the pool with Melody since we were kids. I'm pretty sure I haven't seen her lower back in years." She pinched the crease on the paper to make sure Gabe stayed in there. "How did you make the connection between Melody's tattoo and Chris Contreras?"

"In the same file that contained the photos, there was a list of fingerprints found in the apartment—ours were listed—so were those of some guy named Christopher Contreras. The name didn't ring a bell when I first saw it. Figured it was some friend of hers, maybe someone in the program. Then I saw the tattoo and had a hunch. When I looked up Contreras, saw his rap sheet, saw his photo, I guessed he might be Altamarino."

Jolene clasped her knees with her hands, her nails digging into her flesh. "That would explain why he's still alive, wouldn't it? He must've noticed the other Pink Lady mules' disappearing act and figured a name change would go a long way toward saving his life."

"Exactly. He resurfaces as Gabe Altamarino, starts going out with Melody and keeps seeing her even when Wade tells him to get lost." Sam rubbed his chin. "I just can't figure out how Wade knew about Gabe's criminal past if he were no longer Chris Contreras."

"I don't think Gabe made a secret of the fact that he was a reformed bad boy. Maybe he got in front of that story so Wade wouldn't do any checking on his own and dig up Gabe's real name."

"Gabe must've put together that list of mules he gave Melody for safekeeping, and he probably knows why those mules disappeared." Sam flexed his fingers on the steering wheel. "And he must have some idea how that land is linked to Pink Lady and the disappearances and the casino."

"He's not going to want to tell us, is he?"

"Maybe we won't give him a choice."

"Are you sure you have the right address for him in Tucson? Why would he give an accurate address if he's trying to hide out?"

"He doesn't have a choice about that, either. He's still on parole. His parole officer has to have a correct address for him, or he goes back in the slammer. And if he goes back inside as Chris Contreras…"

"The drug cartel will find him." Jolene bunched her skirt in her hands. "Why did Melody keep seeing him?"

"You know your cousin liked bad boys, right? That's why she handed me off to you. I was on the wrong side of the law for her."

"While I'm glad she handed you off to me, as you so delicately put it, I wish she would've found a good guy of her own."

"I guess the joke was on Melody because I didn't turn out to be such a good guy, after all."

She flashed him a quick glance. Was he fishing for compliments? That wasn't his style.

His tight jaw and turned down mouth told her otherwise. He was still beating himself up for lying about the last time he'd hooked up with his ex.

Who was she kidding? *She* was still beating him up for that. Could she ever stop?

"At least you're on the right side of the law." Jolene bit her lip. That hadn't come out right.

Sam snorted. "At least that."

As they made the drive to Tucson, the sun set

over the desert floor, the scattered clouds creating pink-and-orange streaks across the sky.

Sam talked about San Diego and after some tentative starts, told her more about Jess. She must've given him the impression that she blamed his daughter for their separation. Didn't she? She hadn't wanted to think about Sam with his daughter, but he seemed like a great dad and she liked this side of him. So, she encouraged him this time and learned even more about him as a man and a father.

As the signs began to herald Tucson, Jolene asked, "So, where are we going to find Gabe or Chris?"

"His address is near the university."

"He's not going to want to talk to us."

"Me. I brought you along, but I want you to wait for me someplace public. I'll deal with Contreras."

"That's not gonna work, and you know it, Sam. You're not going to get any information out of him." She held up her hand as he opened his mouth. "I have an idea. Let me finish."

"Go ahead, but I can already tell I'm not going to like this idea of yours."

"Chris knows me, right? Or at least Gabe does. He'll talk to me. I have an excuse to see him. I'll bring him the news about Melody, tell him that she confided in me that they were still a thing.

I'll get him talking. Just tell me what you want to know."

Sam had been shaking his head during her entire speech. "Bad idea. We don't know that he didn't kill Melody. His prints were in her place."

"Gabe didn't have a motive to kill Melody. She loved him and would've done anything for the guy—and he knew it. She defied her brother to be with him on the sly."

Sam flicked on the turn signal to exit the freeway. "Do you think Contreras cares about that? Melody knew too much. She was cousins with you—a woman who wanted to know more."

"You know I'm right, Sam. He's not going to give you the time of day. Let me go in first. You can be close by." She snatched up her purse and unzipped it. She spread it open to show her dad's gun. "I came prepared. I'll be okay."

His eyes widened. "You told me you knew how to use that thing, right?"

"Dad taught me." She zipped up her purse and stashed it at her feet. "If it makes you feel better, I can call you first and leave the line open so you can hear everything that's going on between us."

"That would be dangerous." When Sam ran his knuckles across the stubble on his jaw, she knew she'd hooked him. "I can keep out of sight while you make contact with him. He starts acting aggressive, get out of there. He asks leading questions about the casino project and your interest in it, get out of there. If he's hostile, suspicious—"

"I know." She snapped her fingers. "I'll get out of there. This will work, Sam—better than the law marching in there making accusations."

"We'll see what the setup is first." He hit the steering wheel with the heel of his hand. "Damn, I wish I had a wire or something to listen in—and don't mention leaving the phone line open. Too much could go wrong in that scenario."

A few turns after the freeway exit, and Sam was wheeling through downtown Tucson. A little more wheeling, and they'd be exiting downtown Tucson.

"How close to the campus is he?"

"Close enough to have a thriving street business with the students, if that's his game here. He's in an apartment off Broadway."

Two minutes later, Sam turned onto Broadway itself, the street busy with cars. The GPS informed them they'd be turning right in two blocks.

"Looks like school started or is about to." Sam pulled into a grocery store parking lot and took a spot near the street. "Let's plan this attack. I'll wait here. You take the car, so he's not suspicious. Will he recognize you?"

"Probably." She tossed her hair over one shoulder. "I had shorter hair, but I don't look much different."

His gaze appraised her, and she hoped a blush hadn't accompanied the warmth she felt in her cheeks.

"Then I'll tell him I'm there with news about Melody…or I'll ask him if he heard about Melody because I'm supposed to know they've been seeing each other. I'll explain that I was in town and wanted to make sure he knew what had happened. Will that work?"

"I don't like sending you in there alone."

"I won't be alone." She dragged her purse into her lap and patted it. "I'll have Mr. Smith and Mr. Wesson with me."

Sam rolled his eyes. "Now, I'm really worried. That gun is a Glock."

"Better yet." She hitched the purse over her shoulder. "I'll have Ms. Glock with me."

"Okay, this is where you and Ms. Glock are going." He rattled off the address, and then slipped out of the car.

She followed suit and skirted the rear of the car to get into the driver's seat. Before she got behind the wheel, Sam pinched her shoulders with his fingers. "Be careful."

She stood on her tiptoes and kissed his chin. "I will."

She drove the two blocks to Gabe's house and

pulled right in front, as if she had nothing to fear. Her hand had a slight tremble when she removed the keys from the ignition.

She marched past a typical Tucson front yard—a few scrubby cactus, gravel and a tangle of weeds spilling to the curb. She knocked on the door and held her breath, repeating in her head, *This is just Gabe Altamarino, Melody's boyfriend.*

Blowing out a breath, she knocked again. They hadn't discussed a plan B if Gabe wasn't home, or worse, didn't live here anymore.

The door creaked open, and a man stood framed by the doorway, yawning and scratching his bushy hair. Not Gabe.

"Hi, is Gabe around?"

The man poked his head outside practically over her shoulder, and she got a whiff of sweat and weed. "If you're a student looking to buy, you don't come to the house."

She looked like a college student? She liked this guy—despite the sweat and the weed.

"I'm not a student. Gabe is, was, dating my cousin, Melody. I was in Tucson and wanted to touch base with Gabe."

"Oh, yeah, man. Bad news about Melody. Gabe was destroyed."

Jolene blinked. "I-is he home?"

"Naw, he went to University Ave. to hit up some bars and maybe do a little business."

"Oh." Jolene sawed at her bottom lip. "Do you know which bar?"

"There aren't that many down there. He's in one of them, or you could try coming back tomorrow. What's your name?"

"Jolene. I'll find him on University."

As she drove back to the grocery store parking lot, she decided not to tell Sam that she gave Gabe's roommate her name—just in case that was a stupid thing to do. She pulled into a space in front of the store where she saw Sam leaning against a pillar, drinking a coffee. He had another cup in his hand.

She put the car in Park, and it idled as he placed a cup on the roof of the car and opened the door. "I got you a latte. How'd it go? Not there?"

"I talked to his roommate. Gabe's barhopping on University. I can catch up to him there."

Sam retrieved the cup from the top of the car and ducked inside, placing both cups in the cup holder. "What kind of guy is his roommate?"

"Stoned."

"That makes sense." Sam moved the seat back. "This will make things easier. You look for Contreras in the bars, and I'll tag along after you. Text me when you locate him, and I'll saunter into the bar like a stranger—a stranger who can keep an eye on you. I like the idea of you meeting Contreras in a public place better than holing up with him in his house."

"Oh…" she reversed and pulled out of the lot "…he knows about Melody's death."

"Because he heard or because he killed her?"

She parked the car a block away from University, as they didn't want to chance Gabe spotting them getting out of the same car. Sam waited while she slipped out of the car and strode toward the lights and sounds of the main drag outside the gates of the university.

She didn't have to turn around once. She knew Sam had her back and wouldn't let her out of his sight. She could trust him—for that.

Most of the bars gathered on one side of the street with one big restaurant-bar on the other side, which catered more to the parents of the college students, especially at this time of year. Gabe wouldn't want to show his face there and freak out Mom and Dad.

She tripped into the first bar, had a quick look around and slipped out. A bigger crowd in the next place had her squeezing between groups of students and poking her head into the patio area.

As she left that place, she spotted Sam sitting on a bench sipping his coffee. She looked away and ducked into the next bar where live music blared and frat boys shouted their beer orders to the bartender.

She squeezed her way up the stairs to the balcony that hung out over University. When she reached the top step, she scanned the students starting their school year off with a bang, the boys all male bravado, the girls flexing the power of pouting lips and bared midriffs. A few shell-shocked parents cropped up here and there, and the older hangers-on who flitted around the edges of university life to take advantage of naive girls and profit from misguided boys.

Her gaze skittered to a stop when she located Gabe, one of those hangers-on. She turned from the balcony and sent Sam a quick text that she'd found Gabe.

She smoothed her hands down the front of her denim skirt and launched herself into the fray. She wended her way to the table by the balcony edge, zeroing in on Gabe.

He must've felt her attention, as his head jerked up from his beer and his eyes widened. He half rose from his chair, plopped back down and sent the two boys he was probably scamming on their way.

Approaching his small table, crowded with empty beer bottles, she waved. "Gabe, do you remember me?"

"Yeah, yeah." He coughed a smoker's cough. "You're Mel's cousin."

She indicated the chair. "Can I sit for a minute?"

He shrugged. "Yeah, sure. What the hell are you doing here? H-how's Mel?"

"You don't have to pretend with me, Gabe." She flattened her hands on the sticky table. "I know you two were still seeing each other, and I know you know she's dead. I just talked to your roommate."

His eyes darted to the side and back to her face. He licked his lips. "How'd you know where I lived?"

"Melody." She flicked her fingers, eager to move on. She had no clue if Melody knew Gabe's address here in Tucson or had it in her phone—her missing phone. "I was in town visiting a friend and thought I'd drop by and tell you what happened."

"I heard some homeless guy killed her." He gripped the edge of the table with stubby fingers sporting tattoos on every space before the first knuckle. "That guy who was squatting in the apartment next to hers. I told Mel to rat him out, but she felt sorry for him."

"That was Mel." She shredded the edge of a napkin. "When was the last time you saw her?"

His jaw hardened, and his dark eyes narrowed. "Not sure. You tell the cops about me?"

"No." Now she proceeded to fold the tattered

napkin, unable to keep her fingers still. "No reason to tell them. They got their man."

"You tell her brother Wade?" As he finished pronouncing her cousin's name, his lips stretched into a grimace.

"I didn't tell anyone—not then, not now. Just thought you should know in case you hadn't heard about her death."

"I heard." He gulped down some beer from his bottle and slammed it down on the table.

Jolene flinched. Is that what he wanted? To scare her off?

Not so fast.

"Was Melody doing drugs? I know she'd started drinking again."

He wiped the back of his hand across his mouth. "You blaming me for that?"

"No." She rubbed her sweaty palms on her skirt. Now it was time for *her* gaze to dart, and she did a double take when she noticed a cute coed sidling up to Sam, a bottle of beer clutched in his hand.

When her eyes made it back to Gabe's face, his nostrils flared and his eye twitched. He hunched forward and grabbed her wrist, his tattooed fingers biting into her skin. "What the hell are you doing here, and what do you want from me?"

As Jolene wrenched her arm from his grasp,

a couple of girls squealed behind her and a chair banged to the floor.

Gabe looked up and swore. As Sam swooped down on their table, Gabe launched himself over the ledge of the balcony.

Jolene shot up in her chair and leaned over in time to see Gabe land on top of a canvas umbrella on the restaurant's patio and roll off to the sidewalk.

Sam flew past her and shouted over his shoulder. "Stay here."

He took the same path as Gabe, landing on the same umbrella, now with a little less bounce, and scrambled to his feet to give chase.

The students took the chaos in stride, and a couple were already moving in to claim the prime table. "You leaving?"

"Damn right I am." Jolene snatched up her purse and took the safe route down to the street.

She looked both ways when she hit the sidewalk. Would Gabe run back to his house? Probably wouldn't want to lead Sam back there, but he wouldn't want to be running through campus, either, with the campus police on watch.

She hustled down the street and veered around the next corner. She'd guessed right. Sam was running ahead of her with a weird, halting gait. As she opened her mouth to call out to him, the sound of gunshots cracked through the night.

Sam dropped to the ground and Jolene screamed, her whole world collapsing in front of her. The adrenaline fueled her system, and her legs pumped harder and faster.

When she reached Sam, she crouched beside him. With a sob in her voice, she asked, "Are you hurt? Did he shoot you?"

"I'm fine." Lifting his head, he aimed his gaze down the street. "They got Contreras."

Jolene jerked up her head, noticing Gabe in a heap in the middle of the road. A few neighbors had poked their heads out their front doors, too scared to come outside. She didn't blame them.

"Where'd the shot come from?"

"I saw a car slow down on the block ahead, and I'm pretty sure that's where the shots came from. I don't know why the shooter didn't turn the gun on me or, God forbid, you, but he could circle around."

Jolene rose to her haunches. "Gabe might still be alive. We have to talk to him. These neighbors probably already called the police. I'm not done with him."

As she launched forward, Sam made a grab for her leg and missed. "Jolene, stop."

Her sneakers slapped on the pavement as she ran crouched over toward Gabe's fallen form. As she reached his side, she glanced up to see Sam hobbling after her. Had he lied about getting hit?

Gabe's chest rose and fell with each tortured breath he took, blood spurting from the wound in his chest.

Jolene grabbed his hand and put her face close to his. "What do you know about Pink Lady?"

Gabe gasped, but his lips began moving through the blood.

Sam had reached them, his body coiled and tensed, standing over her, his head swiveling from side to side. He had her back.

She hissed in Gabe's ear as the sirens started bearing down on them. "Pink Lady. The casino property. What do you know?"

"The thumb drive." Gabe choked. "I have a video on the thumb drive. Couldn't touch me. EGV couldn't touch me. Video from the drone."

Gabe's body slumped, and the blood stopped pumping from his chest.

As the red-and-blue lights bathed the scene and the sirens wound down to an echo, Jolene cranked her head around to stare into Sam's face. "The thumb drive? What does he mean?"

Sam raised his dark eyebrows. "Thumb, drum, crumb. Tucker had incriminating video of the casino property—and I'd bet my life it's in the vacant apartment next to Melody's."

Chapter Seventeen

With the police on the scene, a few neighbors had gathered in their driveways. A patrol car squealed to a stop, feet from Sam and Jolene.

When the officer exited the vehicle, hand hovering over his weapon, he shouted, "What happened here?"

Sam tipped his head toward Contreras laid out in the street. Jolene still crouched beside him. "Gunshot victim."

"Did you shoot him?"

Sam raised his hands. "No, we just stumbled onto the scene. When we heard the shots, we hit the deck."

"Is she with you?" The officer pointed his finger at Jolene.

"Yes. It looks like he was hit in the chest and stomach. He was gushing blood, but now it's just pooling around him. He's dead."

The cop's chin jutted out. "You law enforcement?"

"Border Patrol." Sam reached for his back

pocket and flipped out his badge to show the officer.

The EMTs had joined Jolene next to Contreras, easing her out of the way. She sat on the street, knees drawn to her chest and a pair of blood-stained hands wedged on the asphalt behind her.

Sam kneeled beside her. "Are you okay? My heart stopped when you took off for Contreras, but you done good, kid."

Her glassy eyes tracked from the EMTs working fruitlessly on Contreras to Sam's face. "We have to get that video."

"Shh. We will."

She sat forward, bringing her hands in front of her face. "There was so much blood. What did you tell the police?"

"Not much." Sam glanced over his shoulder at the approaching officer. "We heard the shot and saw him fall. You tell the EMTs anything?"

"Nothing…but, I mean nothing." She placed a hand on the ground and struggled to her feet, as the officer hovered over her.

Sam took her arm and helped her up.

"Ma'am, are you all right?" The officer's gaze dropped to her hands, streaked with Contreras's blood.

"I'm fine."

"Are you a nurse?"

"A nurse?" She shook her head. "I just thought I'd see if I could help."

"Did you?"

"No. He was already dead or fast on his way. There was no way to staunch that blood."

The officer had a few more questions for them, and by the time he was finished, Contreras had been pronounced dead. The cop held his card out to Sam. "We have your information, Agent Cross. Now you have mine. If you remember anything about the incident or the car, let us know. The deceased is a known drug dealer in Tucson, so his manner of death is not all that surprising. Ma'am, the EMTs can see to your hands. Are they injured?"

"No." Jolene spread her fingers in front of her, as if just noticing the blood. "Thanks, I'll walk over."

Sam pressed his hand against the small of Jolene's back and steered her to the ambulance, calling out to the EMT. "Do you have some solution to clean off her hands? Murder victim's blood."

"Of course." One of the EMTs ducked into the back of the ambulance and emerged with a clear liquid in a bottle and gauze pads. As Jolene held out her hands, the EMT squirted the solution over her hands and wiped them with the gauze. He did it one more time, removing all traces of Contreras's blood.

The EMT handed her a pristine dry towel. "Are you all right, otherwise?"

"I'm fine." Jolene hopped off the back of the ambulance. "Sam?"

"All good. Let's get back to the car." He took her hand, and they walked down the middle of the street, the residents still gathered in small clusters in driveways and curbside.

Sam tipped his head toward Jolene's. "It came from the car. Did you see it roll by right before the shot was fired? Two shots, one kill."

"I didn't see anything but you running in front of me…limping, like you are now. What happened to your leg?"

Sam squeezed his left quad. "Jammed it up when I jumped from that balcony. Did I overreact? When I saw him grab your wrist…"

"He was gonna run one way or the other." She untangled her hand from his, and wrapped her arm around his waist. "Lean on me if you have to. When you saw Gabe grab my wrist, you couldn't have felt any worse than I did when I watched you crumple in front of me."

"You thought Contreras had turned and shot me?"

"Yes." She covered her eyes with her hand for a second. "Filled me with panic."

"So much so, that you didn't hear me yelling at you to keep down. That car could've made a U-turn and come back at us."

"But it didn't. Much better for a lone drug dealer to get gunned down than three people tied together by one person—Melody Nighthawk."

His shoulder bumped hers as he stumbled. "You figured out that was no random killing or drug deal gone wrong."

"Someone's been watching Gabe…or us. Wanted to keep him quiet…about that video."

"It almost worked."

Jolene glanced over her shoulder before they turned the corner. "What do you think is on the video? It was enough to keep Gabe alive for two years."

"We'll find out. Do you remember when Tucker was babbling about his thumb?"

"Vaguely. He said so much nonsense."

"He said Pinky gave him the thumb drive and that it was in the floor."

Jolene stumbled. "You think it's in the floor of Melody's apartment or the one next door?"

"I think Melody gave it to Tucker to hide in the place next to hers. I just hope it's there and not in some hidey-hole of Tucker's. Maybe she gave the thumb drive to Tucker, maybe not. Maybe he saw her hiding it in her place, in the floor."

"And Gabe… Contreras must've given the

thumb drive to Melody for safekeeping—putting her life in danger."

When they reached the car, Sam pulled out his phone, tapped it and crouched next to the rental.

"What are you doing?" Jolene hovered over him.

"The person who shot Contreras knew we were here to meet him. That means they were keeping tabs on him, or someone is tracking us. I'm going to check the car chassis for a GPS device. We have the capability on our phones now—mandatory after several of our agents were personally targeted by the cartels."

His ears primed for the telltale beep that would signal a device, he continued his sweep, crawling on the ground, waving his phone beneath the car as Jolene followed him, functioning as his lookout just as he'd kept watch when she was talking to Contreras. They made a good team.

Satisfied, he rose to his feet, brushing off the knees of his jeans. "Nothing, which means Contreras was being followed, whether he knew it or not. His name change didn't fool them. They must've been watching him for a while, knew he'd been in contact with Melody. Even though he had that video over their heads, they watched him."

He opened the passenger door and nudged her inside. Then he limped around to the driver's side. As he repositioned the seat, she ran her hand along his thigh.

"Is your leg okay?"

"Just sore. I'll be fine." He laced his fingers with hers and brought her hand to his lips. "We're falling apart piece by piece, aren't we?"

"Nobody else I'd rather fall apart with." She caressed his chin. "I'm glad to have you on my side, Sam—now let's find that thumb drive."

BY THE TIME they got back to Paradiso, it was almost midnight. Once again, Sam pulled into the parking lot of Melody's apartment building. With the car idling, he said, "Maybe we should leave this for the morning."

"Are you crazy?" Jolene released her seat belt. "Melody and Contreras were killed for that video. It's the proof you've been waiting for."

He cut the engine. "Maybe *you* should leave this for the morning. I'll go inside and you can take the car home."

"I'm in this, Sam, just as much as you are." She patted his forearm, tense and corded as he gripped the steering wheel. "I'll be fine. Nobody's going to be here. Nobody followed us, nobody is tracking this car."

He opened his mouth, and she pushed open her door before he could raise any more objections.

She knew he'd been spooked when someone shot at them, but this wasn't the same. Was it?

She skipped across the parking lot before Sam even got out of the car, taking advantage of his bum leg. She did wait for him at the base of the stairs, palming Melody's key. She had every right to be here.

When he caught up with her, he panted. "You don't play fair."

"Can you make it up the stairs okay?"

"Yeah, yeah, let's get going. We don't want anyone seeing us hanging around here."

She jerked her thumb over her shoulder. "Too late. There's a couple standing outside a car in the parking lot."

Sam said, "Then let's do a search of Melody's place first, as you have the key. When they're gone, we'll get into the vacant unit."

They reached Melody's front door, and Jolene unlocked it and stepped over the threshold. Sam crowded in behind her, whispering in her ear, "Don't turn the lights on. We don't want to signal anyone. I've got my flashlight."

Sam snapped the door closed, secured the curtains at the front window and flicked on his flashlight. "We've already searched all the conventional places and didn't see any thumb drive. The cops would've scooped up anything like that. It's time to search the unconventional."

"What did you remember Tucker saying about the thumb drive?" Biting her bottom lip, Jolene peered into the dim, disheveled room. Had someone besides the police tossed the place?

"Besides thumb, drum, crumb?" Sam aimed his light at the tiled floor. "He said the thumb drive was in the floor."

Jolene stamped her sneaker against the tiles. "How can something be hidden under tile?"

"That's what worries me about any information from Tucker. He wasn't exactly rooted in reality." He skimmed the light across the room. "Let's check the closets."

They combed the floors of Melody's apartment, which were tiled throughout. Jolene skimmed her toe across two squares. "This is new stuff, too. No chips or cracks or loose tiles. In fact, I remember Melody talking about how she'd had a water leak that ruined the wood floors and the management company was replacing everything with tile."

"Wood floors?" Sam cocked his head. "Some of these units have wood floors?"

"I know. You could actually hide something beneath wood flooring. Maybe the place where Tucker was hiding has the wood."

Jolene strolled to the wall Melody's place shared with the vacant unit next door. "That would explain why Melody gave Tucker the flash drive—so he could hide it in the floor."

"Then, that's where we need to be." Sam snapped off the flashlight and made a move for the front door. "Is that couple gone now?"

Jolene stepped outside and peered over the railing into the parking lot. "They're gone. How are we going to get in there?"

"Give me some credit. If Tucker Bishop can break into an abandoned apartment, so can I."

Five minutes later, Sam made good on his promise as he picked the lock on the empty unit and pushed open the door.

Jolene held her breath against the musty smell, as she stepped inside the unfurnished unit. "If the cops came in here, they didn't have much to search."

Sam's flashlight lit up a dirty blanket in the corner. "Tucker's bed."

Tapping her toe against the tile floor, Jolene said, "Looks like they replaced this floor, too."

Sam crept to the back of the apartment and called over his shoulder. "Not in the bedroom."

Jolene followed the light and joined Sam in the bedroom, the hardwood floor stretched out before them like a treasure map. Now they just had to find the treasure.

Sam slid open the mirrored closet door and lifted a wooden clothes rod from its brackets. "You use this to tap the floor, and I'll crawl around and use the end of my flashlight. You're listening for a hollow sound or looking for any irregularities in the seams of the floor."

They started in opposite corners of the room, tapping away like a couple of deathwatch beetles. Jolene hit each panel of wood with the end of the rod, cocking her head, listening for different sounds.

She approached the lone window in the room and rapped the end of her stick against the piece closest to the wall. Instead of the light, tinny sound she'd grown accustomed to, she heard a deeper sound. She tapped again and tapped the panel next to the first one.

The dark hollow sound had her heart racing and she dropped to her knees. "I think I found something, Sam."

He was at her side in an instant, the light from his flashlight playing over the floor.

"These two." She ran her fingers along the two panels of wood next to the wall. As she pressed on one side, the wood wiggled. "This is it."

Sam withdrew a knife from his pocket and flipped it open. The blade gleamed in the low light as he inserted it along the edge of the wood. He jiggled it a few times, loosening the piece. He then jammed it into the crease and eased it back, using it as a lever.

The other edge of the wood lifted from the

floor. He worked the sides until it popped up, and Jolene grabbed it.

Sam aimed the flashlight into the small cavity, as Jolene bent over the space. "See anything?"

With trembling fingers, Jolene reached into the dark area and pulled out a thumb drive attached to a long ribbon printed with the pecan-processing plant logo where Melody had worked.

She released a long breath. "It's here."

SAM DROVE TO Jolene's place with her squirming in her seat beside him and his gaze pinned to his rearview mirror. That thumb drive she had squeezed in her fist felt like a ticking bomb to him and the longer they had it in their possession, the greater danger they were in... *Jolene* was in.

When they got to her house, Jolene grabbed her laptop and booted it up at the kitchen table as Sam hovered above her and Chip circled around their legs, sensing their agitation.

She double-clicked to open the thumb drive, and a list of videos popped up, organized by date.

Sam squinted at the dates, which went back about a year. Then he took a deep breath and said, "Let's dive in."

Jolene brought up the first video, which showed drone footage of the Yaqui land slated for the casino. "Why did they have a drone out there?"

"To monitor the area. Make sure nobody was snooping around—like us."

"Or my father."

Sam squeezed her shoulder. "Keep going. I don't see anything incriminating yet."

They studied each video, and Sam noted that most of the coverage was for the border area, along those ridges. Would he have found a tunnel across the border if the shooters hadn't stopped him? What would he have found in that tunnel?

When the next video started, Jolene gasped and jabbed her finger at the screen. "People."

Sam leaned in close but couldn't make out any faces. "They don't seem to be too worried, do they? They're not sneaking around."

The next few videos were more of the same, and then things got interesting.

Sam whistled. "Hello—there's evidence of digging."

"Sam, look at the edge of the display. Two people are carrying a tarp—an old, dirty tarp—and it looks like they're disappearing into the ridge."

"It's a tunnel, just like I thought. They're moving…bodies into that tunnel. They're digging up the mules who were murdered after transporting Pink Lady across the border and stashing them in that tunnel." He tapped the screen. "This is all prior to the studies done on the land. They knew the casino was coming and had their own preparations to do."

Jolene displayed the next video, and the drone zoomed in close to the people this time.

Sam's pulse jumped. "Stop!"

Jolene paused the video. "You know that man?"

"That's Ted Jessup, El Gringo Viejo. We need to put these videos in the hands of the DEA, the FBI, the Pima County sheriffs."

Jolene started up the video again. "I hope the bones are still in the tunnel, but you don't know where Ted Jessup is, do you?"

"No. Wait!" Sam's heart slammed against his chest. "Go back a few seconds."

Jolene dragged back the video that showed Ted Jessup talking with a few other people. A woman. He had his arm draped around the shoulders of a woman.

"Freeze there. Can we zoom in on those faces? That woman?"

After a few false starts, Jolene was able to zoom in on the youthful face of a woman with a long braid over her shoulder, a braid streaked with gray.

"I know that woman. She's Karen Fisher, the representative of the consortium of financers backing the casino. She's here in town, and she's behind everything."

Jolene blew out a long breath. "We have her, Sam. La Gringa Vieja."

Chapter Eighteen

Sam straightened his bowtie in the mirror, and Jolene came up behind him and wrapped her arms around his waist, careful not to smudge the collar of his white shirt with her red lipstick. "Are you sure we're doing the right thing?"

Sam patted the flash drive in his pocket. "We don't know who we can trust right now. I don't want this getting lost or deleted or corrupted. You saw what happened to Tucker in custody where he was supposed to be safe."

"I'm glad we didn't see my cousin Wade in any of that drone footage, but do you think he could be involved?" Jolene dropped her arms from Sam and rubbed the goose bumps that had risen on them.

"Do I think he knew that land was a dumping ground for dead drug couriers? No, but he knew those people wanted access to the land prior to the casino going up—and he gave it to them in exchange for money and support."

"Sounds like something Wade would do." She smoothed the skirt of her glittery white dress over her thighs. "When Rob Valdez's girlfriend, Libby, ID'd Ted Jessup in Rocky Point as El Gringo Viejo, did she mention a wife or a girlfriend? Where did this Karen Fisher come from?"

Sam shrugged, the tuxedo jacket tightening across his broad shoulders. "I don't know, but she and Jessup sure seemed cozy in the videos, didn't they? She's obviously the face of the financial empire EGV has built up with drug money. Jessup made sure to stay away from the public eye."

"We could just turn this information over to the cartels, and they'd handle it in their own way. They don't look too kindly on double-crossers."

"There's been enough bloodshed over Pink Lady, and if we can get Karen in custody, she'll most likely sing like a bird and the DEA and FBI can shut down the production of Pink Lady for good." Sam spun around from the mirror. "Does this look okay? The rental shop didn't have time to do any tailoring."

She trailed her fingers down his lapels. "A little tight across the shoulders, but that just makes you look even more buff."

"Okay, because that's the look I'm going for." He rolled his eyes. "You, on the other hand, look like a shimmery white cloud of perfection. Actually, you look like one of those princesses Jess always wants me to read about. Wait until I tell her I know a real princess."

"When she meets *this* princess, she's going to be extremely disappointed." Jolene caught her breath as Sam grabbed her hand.

"Does this mean you want to meet her?"

Jolene nodded, afraid to speak around the lump in her throat, afraid to ruin her carefully applied makeup with tears.

"Let's get through this, first." Sam pulled her close and kissed the side of her head. "Let's go."

As they drove to Tucson for the casino gala, Sam drummed his thumbs on the steering wheel, running through their plan. "Are you sure the AV guy you know at the hotel is working this gig?"

"He said he was, and if not, he'll give his replacement a heads-up."

"He's not worried about losing his job?"

She jabbed Sam in the side. "If everything unfolds as planned, he's going to be the hero of the evening. He won't have to worry about his job."

"I've put all the other agents who are going to be there on notice." Sam ran the tips of his fingers across his clean-shaven jaw. "Even Nash."

"How'd he react?"

"Nothing surprises Nash. He'll do his job."

When they got to Tucson, they had to drive several more miles into the foothills to the Hacienda del Sol. Sam left the car with a valet.

As they walked into the resort, Jolene pressed her hand against her stomach where the butterflies were flapping their wings furiously. They followed the signs to the ballroom, and when they entered, Sam slipped his hand into his pocket, withdrew the thumb drive and pressed it into her hand.

They'd edited together the most pertinent pieces of the videos—the digging, the relocating of tarps into the side of the ridge along the border and the people behind it all. Thank God, she'd never seen her father on the videos—too recent for him—but she was almost sure now that Dad had discovered that tunnel or those bodies and had paid the price for his knowledge—just like Melody, Tucker, Contreras.

Did Wade know the people he'd been dealing with had murdered his uncle, the man he revered and emulated? He must have guessed.

Jolene spotted the AV setup at the back of the room. Lucky for her and Sam, the gala tonight was supposed to feature a presentation on the Yaqui tribe and their land in the desert, straddling the US and Mexico. The video would still feature that land—just not in the way the backers imagined.

She squeezed Sam's bicep through his jacket. "My guy's here."

As she started across the room with purpose,

Wade touched her shoulder. "Looking beautiful, cuz. I'm surprised to see you here."

"Oh, I've come around. I see the light now." She nestled her hand with the thumb drive in the folds of her dress.

Wade's dark eyes glowed. "Glad to hear it because I just got word on those bones that mysteriously appeared at the construction site."

Jolene blinked. "Oh?"

"Just some dried out bones from an archaeology site, not even from Arizona. Funny, huh? But that means, I'll be announcing tonight that the project is proceeding as planned."

"That's great." She spread her red lips into a smile. "It just may not be proceeding with everyone on board."

She twirled away from him and snatched a champagne flute from a passing tray. Gran wouldn't be here tonight, not her thing, but other tribe members stood in clusters around the room and Jolene headed for one of those groups.

She could feel Wade's eyes drilling into her back and didn't want him to see her talking to the AV guy. As she chatted with family members, she glanced at Wade from the corner of her eye hobnobbing with the mayor and his cronies.

Making her move, she swept up her skirt with one hand and sauntered toward the back of the room. "Derek?"

The man behind several computers looked up. "You're Jolene?"

"Yeah, just like we discussed." She slipped him the flash drive and five hundred bucks.

"Is anyone going to come for me once they realize the approved programming is going to be replaced by this?" He held up the flash drive.

"They'll be occupied with other things."

As she turned, Derek stopped her. "Hang on. I'm going to put this video on my hard drive and give the flash drive back to you. That way, if someone does come back here and tries to stop the video by removing it, you'll have your original."

"You're worth every last penny. I do have another copy at home, but that's a great idea."

"I'm doing it for our mutual friend, not really the money. I owe her." He clicked and dragged and clicked again, and then handed the flash drive back to her. "Done deal."

Jolene slipped the drive into her white beaded evening bag and downed her champagne. No turning back now.

She found Sam just as the lights began to dim, and soft music started to play. Slipping her arm through his, she whispered, "It's all set."

Sam nodded toward Nash, spiffy in a custom-tailored tux, sticking close to Karen Fisher's side. Karen sported a silver sheath, her salt-and-pepper hair braided over one shoulder. She didn't look the part of a murderous drug dealer.

As the hors d'oeuvres circulated and the champagne flowed, the speeches began. Wade announced to a delighted crowd that the bones found at the ground-breaking ceremony were planted and not native to the land.

Sam bumped her shoulder and she replied, "Oh, yeah. Forgot to tell you that."

Wade continued, "The Desert Sun Casino is going to provide jobs and boost the economy, just like the pecan-processing plant did. As proud Yaqui, we will be good stewards of the land and property. Now, to thank the tribe, we put together a video of our heritage and culture to share with you tonight."

Sam put his lips close to her ear. "That's our cue."

They split up, Sam ducking out of the ballroom to reenter near the stage—and near Karen Fisher. Jolene crept along the back wall, returning to the AV center. As Derek handed her a mic, she slipped behind a green curtain.

She watched through a slit in the curtain as Derek clicked on the drone video. She licked her lips and flicked on the mic as the video displayed on screens around the ballroom.

The crowd oohed and aahed at the majestic aerial shot of the desert landscape in all its glory.

As the pink-and-orange streaks of a desert sunset faded from the screen, replaced by footage of the ridge along the border, Jolene began to speak.

"The Desert Sun Casino may come to fruition one day, but that land was used for something else before this project—something sinister. Buried in the sand are secrets, evidence of Yaqui land being used to move drugs and murder the mules in the know."

Shouts went up. Demands to hit the lights and stop the video echoed over the hushed silence of the ballroom. Jolene continued her narrative. When the video displayed Ted Jessup with Karen Fisher directing the relocation of people's remains to the border area, the room erupted.

Jolene took a deep breath, ready to identify the people on the screen, but before she could, shots rang out. People screamed and there was a stampede for the doors.

Jolene dropped behind the curtain, reaching out and tugging on Derek's pant leg. "Get down."

She squeezed her eyes closed and silently prayed that Sam hadn't been hit by any of those bullets. Seconds later, bright lights flooded the ballroom, and Jolene blinked as strong arms lifted her from the floor.

Sam folded her against his chest. "You're all right?"

She peered around his large frame at the stage.

One man was down, and Karen Fisher, blood on her sleek dress, had her hands behind her back and Nash was cuffing her.

Jolene swayed as she grabbed on to Sam's arm. "We did it. Who's the guy on the ground?"

"Karen's security. When she saw her face on that video, her guy tried to hustle her out of the room. Nash stopped him, and the man pulled a gun. The three of us were on him before he even had a chance to aim, so his bullets went into the ceiling and Clay shot him. He's not dead, but Karen Fisher and Ted Jessup are finished."

Jolene rested her forehead against his shoulder. "How'd I do?"

"You killed it."

"And Wade?"

He stroked her hair. "He looked shocked. He may have to answer for some questionable business practices, but I don't think he knew how they'd been using that land and why they were so anxious to have a hand in its development."

"I'm glad. I am." She disentangled herself from his arms and tipped back her head to look into his face. "And I got justice for my father and all the others. That casino, if it goes up, won't be built on lies and secrets."

Sam cupped her face with one hand. "Nothing worth having should be built on lies and secrets."

Epilogue

"How much longer until you move back to Arizona, Sam?" Nash looked up from flipping burgers on the grill.

Sam dragged his attention away from Jolene sitting on the steps of Nash's pool with Jess on her lap. "Rob's gotta be processed out first. Hey, Rob, when are you leaving Paradiso, already?"

Rob Valdez, the youngest agent who'd barely been on the job two years answered without looking up from rubbing suntan lotion on his girlfriend Libby's back. "My transfer to LA should have final approval in a few months. Anxious to get rid of me?"

"Anxious to get back to Paradiso. You're going to be a different kind of busy out there in LA, but that's probably what your career needs right now."

"Yeah, most of my family is in LA, and I'd like to be closer to them."

Libby rolled over and sat up. "Thanks to you and Jolene, I don't have to worry about Ted Jessup coming after me for IDing him anymore, so we're free to go wherever."

Nash's fiancée, Emily, sauntered onto the patio from the house, balancing their son, Wyatt, on her hip. "I wish I'd been at that gala. The look on Karen's face must've been priceless when she saw her mug on that screen. I never liked her, anyway."

Emily took a seat next to Jolene in the pool, and Jess started pinching the baby's toes and squealing.

Clay and his wife, April, jogged across the lawn with their dog, Denali, and Chip at their heels.

April pushed a lock of blond hair from her face. "Are we talking about EGV again? I'd rather forget him. He killed my father and was responsible for the deaths of Libby's mother and Jolene's father. He was a one-man wrecking crew."

Clay told the dogs to Stay and grabbed a beer from Nash's outdoor mini-fridge. "His gal pal Karen sure turned on him fast once the FBI had her in custody."

"I wish I'd been there when they busted down his door." April huffed out a breath and reached for a bottle of water. "Hey, Sam, you want some water?"

He held up a hand and she tossed him a bottle.

Libby sat on the edge of the pool, dangling her

feet in the water. "The casino project is going forward, isn't it, Jolene?"

"It is. My cousin was able to provide some evidence about the financials that helped the DEA, so they're going easy on him. I think he lost the confidence of the tribe, though. They're looking for some new leadership."

"How about you, Jolene?" Nash raised a plate of burgers. "Food's on."

"Yeah, how about you?" Dropping his bottle by the side of the pool, Sam slipped into the water and paddled over to Jess. "The tribe trusted your father, and they'll trust you, especially after you took care of business at the gala."

She made a face. "Not for me."

The others vacated the pool to swarm the food Nash and Emily had set out.

Sam ducked his head under the water and popped up in front of Jess, who squealed and giggled. Sam blew bubbles in the water. "She likes you."

"The feeling is mutual." She tucked a wet lock of Jess's hair behind her ear. "Her mom is okay with your move and the custody arrangement?"

"She's thrilled, Grandma not so much."

"Gamma. Gamma."

Emily traipsed back to the pool, holding out her arms. "Do you want me to get this little one some food?"

"Thanks." Sam scooped up Jess and handed her over to Emily.

As Denali trotted behind them to the table, Jess kicked her legs and yelled, "Chip, Chip."

Jolene laughed. "We're going to have to teach her that not all dogs are named Chip."

"We." Sam pulled up next to her on the step and curled an arm around her waist. "I like the sound of that."

She hung her arms around his neck. "You're sure you want to return to Paradiso? Never mind Rob, California could be better for *your* career."

"I love Paradiso. I love the shifting moods of the desert. I love the pulsating heat and the violent monsoons. But most of all, I love the woman who took me back, the woman who taught me to love this mysterious land like I hope she'll teach my daughter."

She grabbed his face with both of her hands and planted a hard kiss on his mouth. "Lessons start tomorrow."

* * * * *